THE WING COLLECTOR

KRISTI HELVIG

Dark
Edge
Publishing

THE WING COLLECTOR

A Novel By

Kristi V. Helvig

Dark Edge Publishing

The Wing Collector

Copyright © 2017 by Kristi V. Helvig

Book design by Steven Novak

For all the freaks

"Trifle not with humans and their greedy, selfish ways;
By remaining strong and Pure, we will end their wicked days."
—*Book of Faerie*

1

DEAD THINGS

Epping Forest, England
September 8, 6:04 a.m.

I wait for her behind a large oak tree. Cool mist dampens the morning air, yet I feel no chill. I'm too focused. I know how it will unfold; the girl's initial confusion will give way to anger, then fear. Despite what I am about to do, I don't want her scared.

I want her dead.

Killing her is necessary in order to find the One.

Streaks of gold penetrate the woods, and I watch the rising sun with impatience. The less light, the better.

Light, tentative footsteps crunch the dead leaves underfoot. The girl mumbles under her breath, "I don't know why we had to meet so early."

I take a slight step in her direction and a twig snaps.

She peers into the fog. "Matt?" she whispers. "Matt, is that you?"

I step out from behind the tree. "My deepest apologies, but Matt couldn't make it."

She starts to run when she sees the knife, and the crumpled note from her crush—as written by yours truly—slips from her hand. Her back turned to me only makes what I have to do easier.

I WIPE the blood on a cloth that I'll later burn. One down, but many remain. I won't waver. I won't tire. I'll make the world a better place—one freak at a time.

CAROLINA DREAMING

Chapel Hill, North Carolina
September 8, 1:04 a.m.

The scream tore from my throat as I jerked awake, certain someone was in the room with me. Shaking, I bolted upright in bed, the sheets drenched in sweat. I fumbled in the dark for the wastebasket and vomited into it. The room was almost pitch-black thanks to the thick, custom-made shutters that covered the inside of all windows in the house.

"Lila!"

Light flooded the room and I shielded my eyes from the glare. Mom ran to my bed and pushed the hair back from my face. She stared with concern at the stench-filled wastebasket. "Lila, what's wrong? Are you okay?"

I couldn't stop shaking. "I don't know." Had I had a nightmare? My eyes fell on the large rose-quartz crystal in her other hand. "Seriously, is that your idea of a weapon?"

Mom managed a weak smile, her blond hair in frizzed ringlets around her face. "It was the closest thing. She pressed the back of her hand to my forehead. "No fever . . . you're just clammy."

I clutched my blanket around me. "I thought it was impossible for me to get sick."

Her brow wrinkled. "I thought so too. Was it a bad dream?"

I tried, and failed, to grasp at something at the edges of my memory. I shook my head. "I don't know. I can't remember."

Just to be sure, she checked my closet and under my bed with the crystal raised above her head like some kind of hippie warrior. Satisfied that no one lurked inside my room, she pocketed the rose quartz. "I'm worried about you. Do you want me to stay?"

"No, I'm fine, really." For emphasis, I leaned back against my pillow and tugged the blanket up to my chin.

"Okay, but yell if you need anything." She took the wastebasket and lingered a minute by the doorway, concern etched across her face, before she flicked off the light and returned to her room.

The darkness fell heavy around me, enveloping me in a black cocoon. Only the lazy whirring of the ceiling fan overhead masked the silence. I tried to steady my rapid breathing. No one was here in the house aside from Mom and me, same as always. We were safe. I told myself this over and over again for the next few hours until sunrise . . . because I couldn't quite make myself believe it.

3

TICK TOCK

Heathrow Airport, London
August 30

I buckle into my seat, ignoring the chipper flight attendant who acts as if the life vest under the seat can actually prevent death if the plane plummets into the icy Atlantic. Still, a smile creeps across my face at what I've accomplished . . . at what is waiting for me across the pond. I can almost smell them—their rotten souls permeating the air around me.

I don't know why they think they have the right to be here at all. Like they can fool us into thinking they are human. That the hideousness behind their normal-looking exteriors will go undetected for long. Stupid creatures.

The plane lifts into the air and I settle back in my seat, gazing at the splendid morning sky out my window. The countdown has begun, and I am the timekeeper. They think they are better than humans, but I'll show them just how wrong they are.

4

PATIENCE AND OTHER WASTED VIRTUES

September 27
2:13pm

I t takes me almost a month to find the next one. The pace will have to pick up if I have any hope of succeeding. The waiting is the hardest part—double-checking their sub-human status, planning the most effective location for their death, and in this case, neglecting my regular obligations in order to finish the task. No one will notice, though—I've covered my tracks too well.

She makes the mistake of leaving early today. Maybe she senses something is wrong, senses that I'm near. Sadly, in trying to save herself, she leaves herself vulnerable—walking home alone by a creek. Tsk, tsk. And to think they consider themselves smarter than humans.

Such pretty wings, though. I have plans for these. My glee is barely contained as her blood soaks into the water . . . and her life *ebbs to nothingness. Not just because I've taken out another one, but because I feel closer to . . . the One.*

OF ALL THE *mutants I will kill, none will compare to the One.*

VOMIT REVISITED

September 27
2:13 p.m.

The way they stared, you'd think they had never seen a girl run before. More likely, it was that they'd never seen *me* run. Maybe the quiet girl charging through school as if her life depended on it did warrant some attention. Still, I didn't appreciate the amusement I saw on their faces. Or the laughter. Though I had no idea what was happening to me, it felt like death was a distinct possibility.

"What's up, Kincade, they givin' away free calculators in class today?" one boy yelled.

Ignoring him, I raced down the hallway, my footsteps echoing against the tile. The wrenching sensation in my stomach increased, propelling me faster. I threw open the girls' restroom door and darted inside. My gut lurched as I locked the stall.

What the hell is going on? Sweat beaded on my forehead. Bending over with my head hovering over the toilet, I focused on the cracked floor tiles as I gagged, a stream of bile erupting from my mouth. *Gross.* Maybe it was the eggs I had for breakfast; maybe they'd gone bad. The irony wasn't lost on me that I might have kept myself safe all these years, only to die of food poisoning.

Get a grip, Lila. I'd heard about stomach viruses—had even seen one of my classmates puke—but I'd never experienced it for myself. I was supposed to be immune to illness —one of the few perks of being me—yet I'd puked twice in as many months. Though it was still difficult to muster much empathy for most of my classmates, I had to admit this sucked.

At the sound of the homeroom bell, I attempted to stand. I put a hand on each side of the stall, partially covering a scribble proclaiming *Lexie was here.* Different colored writing underneath inquired, *Where hasn't she been?*

Relief washed over me as the wave of sickness passed. I stumbled to the sink and splashed cold water on my face, then reached over my shoulders to make sure the bindings hadn't slipped. As much as I hadn't wanted my "extra parts" discovered, not vomiting in the hallway of Northeast High had taken priority. The wayward hair staring back at me from the mirror would have to wait. Only one more class to go. I hurried out the door toward my locker.

THE BELL SIGNALED the start of Ms. Gable's Advanced Algebra, or AA, as nerds like me called it. It was my absolute favorite class. I pressed my fingertip against the pencil point to ensure adequate sharpness, a satisfied smile on my lips.

Some girls might be obsessed with boys or shoes, but my obsession involved numbers. Why shop when you could find the unknown variable in a complex equation?

Although my classmates complained that algebra had little value in the real world, they didn't have a clue. There was inherent perfection in numbers. Something was either right or wrong—no pesky shades of gray.

I shifted in my seat, my bindings already damp from the humidity still hanging in the warm autumn air. It was marginally better than the thick heat of August—North Carolina summers were brutal, and wreaked havoc on both my hair and my bindings. When I looked up toward the front of the classroom, the empty teacher's desk stared back. Weird. Ms. Gable was never late.

Giggling erupted behind me.

"Seriously, did you see Jackie's pants? I mean could her ass look any bigger?"

Miranda. Miranda thought anyone who weighed over a hundred pounds belonged on laxatives.

"Speaking of the fashion-challenged . . . ," Miranda continued, then thankfully dropped her voice to a whisper.

Even though I could no longer hear her, when Glen, the big football jock with an even bigger mouth, laughed the loudest, I knew who they were talking about. He never let an opportunity pass if it involved harassing me. His voice echoed through the classroom. "What a nerd."

What a jerk, I wanted to say, but didn't—I never did. Instead, I shrank in my seat, cheeks burning. My ever-present hoodie was a precautionary measure rather than a lack of fashion sense, but Miranda couldn't know that.

Trendy tops didn't provide adequate wing coverage.

I spotted Ms. Gable outside the classroom speaking to the assistant principal, Mr. Turner. Or maybe flirting, judging by the way she flipped her hair. *Great.* This gave everyone more time to dissect my fashion faux pas. All I wanted was to tackle another formula—insert more numbers into their proper place.

"Seriously, I'm dying here. My mouth tastes like twice-baked cardboard. Anyone got any gum?" asked a boy in the back of the room.

Miranda giggled. "Ash, Ms. Gable will just make you spit it out. She doesn't do gum."

Ash? I remembered hearing something about a new kid this week but hadn't paid attention beyond that.

Another girl whispered loud enough for everyone to hear, "*I'd* give you some if I had any."

A boy called out. "I'm sure he knows you'd give him way more than gum, Lexie." The class broke out in laughter.

Ms. Gable poked her head through the door. "That is quite enough! Get out your homework—and no conversing." She pulled the door shut again.

I bent to retrieve my homework from my bag, proud of the neatly printed equations that filled the page. That's when I saw them—my roll of spearmint breath mints. I wasn't sure what made me do it. Maybe it was the relief of feeling better. Maybe being sick had made me realize I was more like humans than I cared to admit. Whatever the reason, I popped one into my mouth and turned with the roll in my hand.

"I have a mint," I said, searching for the boy who'd spoken.

"Good God, she actually speaks," I heard from one corner of the room. Several girls snickered.

"You're an angel," said the voice.

I bit my tongue to keep from responding. *No, just a faerie.* Technically, a half-faerie, not that it mattered. We were hated by humans every bit as much as our full-fledged relatives. After everything that had happened during the Faerie Wars, it was surprising that Disney had thought it was a smart move to put out a few movies that depicted faeries as cute and mischievous. There had been severe backlash—angry parents protesting outside the theaters, accusing Disney of "normalizing evil."

I twisted my head farther and spotted him in the last row, four seats behind me and over a row. He glanced toward the door, then crept through the aisle until he reached my side, kneeling at my desk. I looked over into the greenest eyes I'd ever seen. His dark hair flopped down just shy of his eyes as he peered into mine. How had I not noticed him before? My ability to speak evaporated, and the fact that his hand was outstretched to accept the mint escaped me.

A slow grin spread across his face. My wings pushed against their restraints, trying to flutter. It took the sound of the classroom door opening for me to regain my senses.

"Sorry—here," I muttered, and dropped several mints into his hand.

"Thanks. I'm Ash, by the way." He turned to rush back to his seat.

"Well, Mr. Cooper, are you introducing yourself to each person individually, or is Lila Kincade just one lucky girl?" asked Ms. Gable.

"No, sorry, Ms. Gable," he responded.

The heat in my cheeks intensified and spread all the way down to my neck. *Pay no attention to the tomato-colored girl in front of you.*

"Good. Well then, let's begin," said Ms. Gable. "Who would like to take us through the first equation?"

I attempted—and failed—to distract myself with the

numbers Ms. Gable wrote on the board. Although I faced the front of the room like the good student I was, Ash's green eyes flashed more than once through my mind. I was pretty sure that made me pathetic.

Of one thing I was very sure. In my entire life, my wings had never reacted the way they had when Ash looked at me.

I was in trouble.

6

OF BLOOD AND WINGS

Pain racked my body on the walk home from school. My back, always swollen and sore by the time the bindings were removed, would be extra raw tonight. Thanks to Ash and the mad beating of my heart in math class, my wings had kicked into high gear and hammered against me nonstop. The humidity hadn't helped either—my wings felt sticky, like they were coated with glue.

"Lila, wait up!" Sophie called from behind. She jogged up next to me, then bent over so she could catch her breath. "Geez, you walk fast. Wanna study for the chem exam?"

I glanced over at my best friend. Even after running, her enviable smooth blond hair looked just the same as it had first period, not a frizzy mess like mine.

"Can't right now, but we can quiz each other tonight on the phone." All I could think about was the pain and getting free.

Sophie frowned but nodded. She'd stopped bugging me as much about coming over to her house, and long ago had given up on asking me to sleep over. There was no way I could stay bound all night without enduring intense pain.

Though we'd been best friends for almost all of our sixteen years, I wasn't sure that would be the case if she knew the truth.

"Okay, but we'll hang out this weekend, right? I want to see *Hacksaw*."

I shivered. "Ugh, the one where the guy in the mask terrorizes the cheerleaders? You always like he creepy movies. What about the one where they guy loses his earm in a freak accident, then falls in love with his nurse? It looks so romantic."

Sophie made a fake gagging sound. "More like looks so lame." Her face brightened. "We could do a double feature, though. Think of all the popcorn we can eat!"

"That's fair . . . but I might have my eyes closed during your bloodbath movie." Normally, I stayed home all weekend to get some relief from the bindings, but being around Sophie made me feel almost normal, so it was worth the pain.

I inhaled deeply while staring up at the towering trees that lined the road. Focusing on the leaves, I tried to distract myself from my agony. I wished I could stop hiding my wings, but I couldn't even imagine what life was like before the Hiding. It was all I knew, though I still wasn't convinced bindings were even necessary, as the boys focused more on my front side. I tried explaining to my mother that if I let my wings fly free but wore a low-cut blouse, the boys wouldn't even notice the extra appendages.

But Mom said it was the girls I had to worry about—that girls can be the cruelest of all.

"Watch out ye young maidens," a voice yelled from behind us. "Passage on your left."

Sophie stepped closer to me as Curtis whizzed by on his skateboard.

"You're weird, Curtis, you know that, right?" Sophie called after him.

Not slowing down, he turned over his shoulder and grinned. "I'll take that as a compliment, milady. Fare thee well." He tipped an imaginary cap toward us and continued onward.

Sophie shook her head.

"You didn't have to call him weird," I said. "He's just . . . different."

Sophie shrugged. "Well, someone has to tell him it's not the 1500s anymore."

We reached the crossroads at my street. "Later, Sophie. I'll call later to quiz you, so be ready."

"I'll be ready, oh smart one." She tossed her hair and pulled her backpack up over her shoulder with emphasis. "In fact, one day, I might even beat you on a test."

MOM READ my face the moment I walked in the door. "You poor thing." She only worked part-time, doing mindless clerical work at a doctor's office, to ensure she would be home by the time school ended each day. She used to work as a nonprofit executive, but claimed she'd been excited to give up the hectic schedule when I came along.

The scent of burning incense wafted through the house. She believed the daily ritual cleansed the energy around us. I wasn't sure it did anything other than make the house smell like patchouli, but it made her happy. She motioned for me to follow her. "Come to your room," she whispered.

"Mom, you don't have to whisper. There's no one else here." As I followed her down the hall, a fresh bout of pain tore along my spine. I placed my messenger bag at the foot of my perfectly made bed—the bag caused less stress on my shoulders than a backpack—then yanked my hoodie off, followed by my shirt, and tossed them on the chair.

"You know we can't be too careful," she said. She pulled on the athletic tape with gentle tugs.

I shifted from one foot to the other. "Just rip it off, Mom. They want out *now*."

She placed her hand on my wings to protect them, and peeled off the tape in one swift motion. Before she could remove the fabric that covered my back, my wings snapped open, ripping the material. They looked like faceted crystal, but were pliable enough to bend like accordions back against my body when necessary. I unwound the rest of the material from around my waist. My wings fluttered in relief, spreading out behind me.

"That feels unbelievably awesome," I said. The area of my upper back where the wings joined my body felt raw. Mom removed a shredded piece of binding from one of the wing tips and smoothed cream around the skin at the base of each wing.

I stretched, arching my back, as a beam of light slipped through the edge of the blinds. The light reflected off my diamond wings, and a cascade of brilliant rainbows danced on the walls.

Mom shielded her eyes. "They seem brighter than usual today."

I yawned. "Really? I hadn't noticed."

She studied my wings. "Definitely." She sighed, brushing a strand of dark hair back from my face. When I was younger, she used to joke that she couldn't wait for the world to see my thousand-carat wings. She'd stopped joking about it years ago. I guess reality had set in. "I wish I could promise you that things will be different someday."

I shrugged. "You can't promise something like that." I scooted into my bed, and pulled out my laptop to start my homework. "You *can* promise me a spaghetti-and-meatball dinner, though."

Mom chuckled. "You know you have a perfectly good desk over there, right?"

I glanced at the surface of my desk. Every square inch was taken by my snow globe collection, carefully arranged in alphabetical order by city name. If I couldn't travel freely and see the world, I'd bring the world to me. I gestured toward my desk. "And where would I put all those?"

"Good point." She gestured at my glowing wings. "I'm off to make dinner, but you'll have to eat in here."

"Yeah, we wouldn't want nosy Nellie seeing me." Our elderly next-door neighbor, Nellie Nesbaum, was super inquisitive, but didn't have the adequate vision and hearing to back up her investigative tendencies. Her true calling in life might have been detective work, but that was hard to do with a Miracle Ear. Still, the light reflecting off my wings was dazzling—even Nellie might notice the high wattage through the kitchen blinds.

After Mom left, I pulled up my algebra homework on the laptop. Reveling in the feel of the air on my wings, I listened as she rummaged through the pots and pans.

As a little kid, I hadn't understood why I had to hide them. Mom had explained that whereas some creatures, like cockroaches, were hated for their ugliness, faeries were resented for the beauty of their wings and the fact that they could fly. The wings reminded humans of what they lacked. After the Hiding, most faeries, though not all, covered their wings for protection. Now that I was older, I knew the Hiding had more to do with the Faerie Wars, but Mom didn't like to talk about it.

I worked on equation after equation, stopping just to sharpen my pencil, and immersed myself in the numbers, only thinking about Ash once. Maybe twice. As I completed the last problem, Mom brought in dinner and set it on the nightstand. "I could join you."

I bit off a piece of the warm garlic bread. "Thanks, Mom, but I have a ton of other homework to do."

She sighed. "Fine, I'll check back on you later. And before bed, I'm going to smudge your room to see if we can keep those nightmares out of here."

I knew better than to argue with her about the efficacy of sage, so I nodded in agreement. After she left, I really tried to concentrate on my English Lit homework, but my mind wandered back to a certain pair of green eyes. After staring at the lilac walls for a few moments, I looked down and noticed I'd doodled Ash's name on my paper. *Perfect.* I could picture it now: Ms. Gable looking at my homework through her blue-rimmed glasses, saying, "Really, Lila, I had no idea that $3x + 2(1/5)y = $ Ash. Care to enlighten the class on this groundbreaking new formula?" I blushed at the thought and shook my head. *Focus, Lila, focus.*

Maybe if Mom hadn't been so protective of me in childhood, I'd have had more normal interactions with boys. Then I would know what to do and could act cool, instead of like a complete idiot. My eyes fell on the T-shirt I'd tossed carelessly over the chair. Frowning, I grabbed the offending garment and shoved it in the hamper where it belonged. This boy was already messing up my neat room and he hadn't even been here. I glanced at the clock, shocked to see how much time I'd spent daydreaming instead of working, and buckled down until every assignment was finished.

Two hours later, I placed the homework in my backpack, the folders color-coded and organized by the order of my classes the following day. Sophie might joke about my OCD, but the last time she couldn't find her homework, she'd asked about my system. As if on cue, she texted me.

Sup, we gonna study chem or what?

Tomorrow. I'm wiped.

K. L8tr gator.

Too wired to sleep, I went online to my favorite book-marked page. Winged, a boutique for faeries, popped up with super cute custom-made tops that even Miranda would appreciate—aside from the holes in the back for the wings. Faeries with wings of all colors posed as though they didn't have a care in the world. They were so brave.

I'd heard some faeries in big cities like London and New York had come out of the winged closet, so to speak, but it didn't seem safe to me. Discrimination was rampant in smaller towns. Even Chapel Hill, which was considered progressive for a Southern city, and supposedly housed a faerie colony, might as well be rural Mississippi in terms of prejudice against nonhumans. Mom said it wasn't safe to come out here, and being that I'd never seen a faerie out in the open anywhere near the Triangle area, I believed her. Someday. Someday I would wear one of those tops. I ran my finger over a fitted pink top on the screen and sighed, then closed the page.

Still curious about my brief bout with illness earlier that day, I clicked to the search engine and typed *can faeries get sick?* I'd always assumed the answer was no, since I never had been. Maybe there was a logical explanation for every-thing . . . I frowned at the results that popped up on my screen. There were gobs of crazy stories by people who claimed faeries had abducted them and performed various bodily experiments. Others were by religious groups claiming faeries were "Satan's soldiers." It would be funny if it weren't so scary. I scanned the page, but couldn't find anything about illnesses, so I tried searching for *faerie viruses* instead, and clicked the Next button.

Halfway down the page, a heading that read *Authentic Faerie Wings* jumped out at me, and the hairs on the back of my neck stood up as I clicked through to the official eBay website. Fear turned to shock when I clicked on the entry.

The screen filled with a photograph of iridescent yellow wings covered in what could only be blood. The item description read *Getting rid of the virus known as fairies, one set of wings at a time.* My heart skidded in my chest. There was only one way for those wings to have been separated from the body: the faerie's seracord—the critical vein running through the center of the wings—had been severed. That was a faerie's lifeline. A faerie couldn't live without its wings any more than a human could live without a heart. Even worse—the wings had been put up for auction only a few minutes earlier, and the bidding had already reached $200,000. Blood roared in my ears. There was even a Buy Now button with a cool one mil price tag.

I'm wrong. It has to be some sick joke. I searched again see if there were other faerie parts up for bid. Several pewter faerie figurines were listed, along with various Tinker Bell trinkets. There, in the midst of those innocuous Disney listings, sat the photo of the bloody wings. I clicked on the wings again, feeling a morbid curiosity as to what others felt my life was worth. It was gone. The listing had been removed less than five minutes after it had been posted. Either eBay had removed it, or the seller had gotten their million. I shuddered.

All the sage smudging in the world wouldn't help me to sleep. I considered telling Mom, but she would freak out. I flipped off the light and tried to rest, but only tossed and turned instead.

The sound of crying got me out of bed sometime later. I tiptoed out of the room and crept down the hallway, my wings flapping behind me, making a soft clicking sound. The muted drone of voices from the television became clearer as I reached Mom's room. I could tell it was the late-night news. Mom's sobs grew louder. My wings started to beat faster, and I stepped away from the wall so the thumping wouldn't give me away.

I peeked around the corner into Mom's room and saw the *Breaking News* banner on the television. The picture of the bloody faerie wings from eBay loomed behind the anchorwoman. Good news traveled fast. The picture faded and was replaced by that of a girl who looked to be about my age. The anchorwoman spoke:

"In possibly related news, a student at Northeast High was reported missing today by her parents. Constance Powers hasn't been seen since leaving for school this morning. Her parents have come forward and acknowledged their daughter was a faerie in Hiding. They have seen the photo and believe the wings belong to Constance. Police have declined to make a statement at this time."

I covered my mouth to keep from screaming. That was my school.

7

PRESENTS FROM PSYCHOS

I lay wide awake, staring at my ceiling. This couldn't be happening. The girl's name and face were familiar, though I hadn't known her. It was crazy to me that someone else with wings had walked through the halls of our school. No matter how many faeries were supposedly nearby, I still felt so alone. There were online forums for faeries, but my mom had warned me that they were traps. And it's not like we could have real-life meet-up groups or anything—faerie gatherings would be way too dangerous— so I hadn't ever had contact with anyone of my kind. That I knew about anyway. It made me wonder: were there more faeries at Northeast?

Tears streamed down my cheeks at the unfairness of it all. Even though there had been warnings about what could happen if a faerie came out of Hiding, I hadn't wanted to believe it. We were blamed and hated for the transgressions of our ancestors, which made us pariahs in this world. Since faeries technically weren't human by legal standards, I bet this girl's death wouldn't even be considered murder. I was surprised it had made the news; the cops likely wouldn't consider it any worse than swatting a fly.

The glowing green numbers on my clock read 3:15 a.m. Less than three hours until I had to get up for class. I stared at the clock until the numbers blurred.

THOUSANDS OF STARS *twinkled like glitter in the sky. I soared among them as the wind blew my hair in tangles around my face, but I didn't need sight to get where I was going. My wings were strong and sure. As I flew over the crest of a mountain, night disappeared in an instant. The sun reflected off a vast ocean, and I shielded my eyes from the dazzling light. A beach filled with soft white sand beckoned in the distance. Faeries danced in the air, laughing as they flitted along the sand or dove toward the water to skim the surface. I would finally meet my own kind.*

I flew toward them as fast as my wings would go, my heart filled with joy. So close now—I could see the translucent hue of each faerie's wings. The one closest to me had pale pink wings, the one next to her, sea-foam green. I opened my mouth to shout a greeting, but the words died in my throat. I watched as an unseen force tore the green wings off the faerie nearest the shore. Wingless in the air, the faerie's body hovered a moment as the blood poured out of her, and she fell limp into the water below. Whatever had killed her worked at a frenzied speed. The faeries barely had time to react.

Several tried to flee, but their wings were torn midflight. Others yelled at me to help, but I hung frozen in the air. I couldn't move. The white sand was now stained blood red as bodies washed ashore. My wings, still paralyzed, refused to propel me away from the carnage. The pink-winged faerie closest to me was the last to die. The screaming stopped. The sun dipped below the horizon. Where there had been light and laughter, there was now only silence. As darkness fell, a looming shadow crept over me....

I WOKE WITH A START, relieved to see the familiar sight of my room. The macabre images floated through my mind again, so I pulled up my online album to replace the bad pictures with good ones. Some early photos of Mom and me—one of mom making a silly face made me smile—but none of the man that she'd been married to before I came along.

I couldn't really blame Mom's ex. After all, he was human, just like Mom, and I wasn't. Unless I had been an immaculate conception, he would have arrived at the same conclusion I had. Mom had cheated with a faerie. Not only cheated, but defied government laws prohibiting human-faerie mating. It was surely quite the shock when I tumbled into the world with tiny wings on my back.

Inhaling deeply, I closed the laptop and went downstairs. On the surface, it appeared to be a day much like the one before: scrambled eggs on the table, bacon sizzling on the griddle, Mom's insistence that I eat protein before school, and the tedious wing-binding ritual.

Though I didn't love being bound, I relished the structure and routine. But today was different. I sat impatiently in my bra and jeans, my back toward Mom. Mom carefully folded the wings against my body. She put the tight mesh fabric over them and taped it in place. Next, she crisscrossed light cotton wrap over my shoulders and tied it around my waist—an extra layer of precaution. If I hadn't been paying attention, it might not have registered that she used an extra row of tape or spent a minute longer than usual smoothing it down.

I waited for Mom's daily, "Be careful, sweetie," as I pulled on my shirt and hoodie.

Instead, she touched my arm as she handed me the backpack. She must have smudged sage on the strap because it reeked. "Lila, be careful. Not everyone is as good as you are."

"Careful is my middle name, Mom," I said. "It's what I do." I struggled to keep my face neutral. Although I was scared, fear was something Mom couldn't handle. She seemed to believe that if she just burned some incense or reorganized her crystals, the problem would go away. Mom and denial were BFF's. Before she could offer me a ride to school, I bolted for the door with the excuse that I was meeting Sophie at the corner.

I dashed to my locker for my chemistry book for first period with Mr. Birchester. Electrons didn't do it for me the way numbers did, so I liked the days when chem was first and I could get it out of the way. Plus, it meant that AA was after lunch, so I had something to look forward to. Anything to take my mind off last night. I spun the knob as I dialed the combination. Despite my way with numbers, or maybe because of it, one of my worst nightmares had been forgetting my locker combination. Now nights filled with unopened locker dreams would be the good ones.

"Hey," said a voice next to me. I jumped. Several textbooks tumbled out of my locker onto the floor. "Sorry," he said, leaning down to retrieve the fallen books.

I couldn't believe I was such a clumsy doofus. *Ash Cooper is speaking to me—again.*

Ash shoved my books back into the locker, then

slammed it shut and turned to me. "I just wanted to say thanks again, you know, for the mint. It's Lila, right?"

I took a deep breath and willed myself to speak.

"Yeah, no big deal. It's just a mint. And you're Ash, the new kid?" My eyes were drawn like magnets to his, and I already felt the twinges in my bound wings.

He gave me a slow smile, which didn't help the whole wing situation. "Yep, that's me. Day three."

My wings beat furiously at their bindings. The bell rang, and everyone started the mad dash for their classrooms. Everyone except us.

"Well, I should go. I'll be late for class." Despite my words, I hadn't moved a muscle.

He glanced down at a printed schedule in his hand. "I'm still figuring out this rotating schedule thing. Okay, it's Wednesday, so we have lab first." He looked up from the schedule at me. "How 'bout I walk with you to Birchester's class?" he asked.

My eyes grew wide. "How'd you know I'm in that class?"

Ash laughed, shaking his head. "Because *I'm* in that class, and obviously in Gable's algebra with you too," he said as he counted on his fingers. "Oh, and we can't forget English lit."

Holy crap . . . he's been in multiple classes with me and I haven't noticed him. What the frick is wrong with me?

He glanced at me. "What? You look surprised." One corner of his mouth turned up in a half smile. "Hey, don't feel bad. Although most people do tend to notice the new guy. What's up with that?"

I swallowed hard. "I . . . I'm pretty focused on my classes. I'm not a big socializer."

He laughed. "Yeah, you are a *pretty* quiet girl."

My face flushed. Had he emphasized the word pretty or

had I imagined it? I searched for a cute response but came up blank.

Ash's eyes swept over my face and back to my eyes. "It's okay. You're a front-row kind of girl and I'm a back-row kind of guy."

I flashed him a shy smile as we walked down the hall together. By the time we reached the lab, we were no longer *going* to be late. We were late.

Sophie's eyes widened when she saw me walk in with Ash.

"Look who's decided to grace us with their presence," said Mr. Birchester. "Lila, as this is most unusual behavior for you. I can only assume that this young man is to blame." He looked over his eyeglasses at Ash. "Ashton, I'll excuse this incident as you're new to the school, but I don't tolerate tardiness in my class. Understood?"

"Yes, sir," he answered. Ash's response was serious, but I heard the smile in his tone.

"Good," Mr. Birchester said. "I hope everyone is studying for the exam this Friday. It won't be an easy one.

The class groaned while Ash took his seat in the back of the room. I sat near the front with my lab partner, Jacinda, and willed my wings to calm down. If it weren't for the fact that I wore a loose shirt covered by the hoodie, the movement of my bindings would totally be noticeable.

Sophie grinned at me from across the aisle and flashed a thumbs-up sign. I'm sure she would have plenty to say after class, but it would be a welcome distraction from thoughts of bloody wings.

Once we got going on our experiments, it didn't take long for the gossip to start.

"Did you see the wings on the news last night?" a girl

behind me whispered to her lab partner while dipping her pH strip into a vial of pond water.

"Yeah, ugh, it was so gross—all that blood."

"Can you believe that girl from Northeast is a faerie?" one boy asked.

"More like *was* a faerie. She's dead," another girl said in a detached voice.

I shuddered and tried not to think about the blood splatter I'd seen at the base of the wings where they'd been hacked off.

A girl in the back of the class waved her pH strip in the air, whining, "My reading is all jacked up. Is this even possible?"

Mr. Birchester walked back to the girl. "Did you add the acidic base?"

"Oh, yeah, forgot that part," she said, reaching for another vial.

"Dumbass," a boy responded.

I tried to tune everything out but my mind was reeling. Voices were everywhere. Out of the corner of my eye, Sophie was waving to get my attention, but I focused hard on the experiment in front of me.

Sam, the boy at the table in front of me, turned to his lab partner, Jake, who also happened to be dating Jacinda. "I thought faeries were super hard to kill or some crap."

That's a total myth.

When both boys turned around, gaping with open mouths, I realized I'd said it out loud. Jacinda looked at me in disbelief and then exchanged a glance with Jake before murmuring, "Dang girl, I've only heard school stuff come out of your mouth before."

Yeah, well I also threw a T-shirt on my chair, so I'm turning all kinds of wild and crazy.

Jake nodded in my direction. "How do you know?"

Though I usually took pride in being honest—as honest as possible, anyway, given my situation—I formulated a lie. "Um, I just read a lot about it for a paper I wrote."

It was only a half lie really, because I *had* read about it, just not for a paper. It was about what the full faeries—Pure Ones—had done during the Faerie Wars two hundred years ago that prompted government backlash: the Pure Ones were ordered to either go back to their realm or face execution.

The other kids looked at me expectantly. Sophie must have heard too, because she was leaning across the aisle. I glanced at Mr. Birchester, who was occupied with another table near the back of the class. I hesitated before adding, "The Pure Ones who refused to go were harder to kill, but the government took care of them—"

"Hell, yeah," said Jacinda. "Damn straight, after what they did."

I swallowed. "So the only kind left here—the ones who went into Hiding—are just half-faeries."

And not many of those, because most people didn't want to associate with faeries, let alone breed with them—even without the anti-mating laws. I'd once heard a rumor that there were rare cases of faerie-worshipping humans, dubbed *faerophiles*, but I found it hard to believe many humans would willingly associate with freaks like us.

Jacinda raised an eyebrow. "I get that Pure Ones were the bad ones, but they should have sent all the freak faeries back, if you ask me."

Jake spoke up. "But they can't. The half-ones have wings and can fly, but only here on Earth where they were born. They don't have the magic of Pure Ones, so they can't travel across dimensions to whatever faerie world they come from."

I stopped myself from nodding in agreement, as Jacinda huffed. "Boy, when did you get all expert on all things faerie? I've asked my parents about this stuff, but it's like they're afraid to talk about it."

Jake shrugged. "My mom told me that's why the government allowed the half ones to live, as long as they agreed to be registered . . . and go into Hiding."

A girl leaned over from across the aisle. "They're not all Hiding anymore. My sister Tabitha goes to Carolina. She has a roommate whose sister's best friend's cousin swears she saw a faerie over at the corner of Franklin and Kenan last summer, wings and all."

"Can I presume that all of this chitchat is about your discoveries regarding the pH levels of your water?" Mr. Birchester asked, stopping next to me in the aisle. I felt his gaze burning into the back of my head.

The girl across the aisle straightened up in her seat and peered down at her water like it was the most fascinating thing she'd ever seen. Jacinda and I bent our heads together and started copying down the acidity levels onto our assignment sheets. The class bell rang and several kids bolted for the door.

"Turn those assignments in before you leave, and I'll expect nothing but perfection from these tables right here." Mr. Birchester gestured toward me before striding back to his desk.

Ash waited at the back of the room, and Sophie hustled to my side. Jake and Jacinda called out to me as I reached Ash.

"Wait up," said Jacinda. "I wanna hear more about this stuff."

We huddled outside the classroom door, and Sophie ran up to us, looking accusatory. "What was that all about in class? You guys have been holding out on me."

Ash flashed me a quizzical look. He clearly hadn't heard my classroom revelations. "I was just telling them about a book I read . . . um, about faeries," I mumbled.

I didn't elaborate, but *Confessions of a Faerie* was penned by Ella Tatiana, a famous half-faerie who came out of Hiding to write a tell-all memoir. Mom said that before I was born, the book was banned by the government and removed from bookstores and libraries, yet I received a pirated copy for my fifteenth birthday. She thought I had the right to know about my kind. The author is supposedly some kind of hermit now, due to all the hate crimes.

Jacinda thrust her hand on her hip. "All I know is the Pure Ones were total a-holes and had it coming."

Ash's jaw clenched. "It's just a shame the half-ones were punished too."

"So that's why they started binding their wings?" Jake asked.

I nodded, my chest tight. "Yeah, so they'd look like everyone else."

Jake let out a low whistle. "Well, if those wings on TV last night were the real deal, they were pretty cool. Of course, not as cool as you," he said, giving Jacinda a quick peck on the cheek.

Jacinda beamed and grabbed his hand. They turned to walk down the hall together, and Jacinda called back over her shoulder, "See y'all."

"See ya," I said.

"Hey," said Ash, "I gotta do something before lit. I'll meet you there, okay."

"Sure, okay," I said, watching him walk away. Had I scared him with my faerie talk?

Sophie punched my arm lightly. "Don't think I didn't notice you and cute boy walking into class together. There's so much you're not telling me lately." She tried to look mad but broke out into a huge smile. "Way to go, by the way . . . you better spill everything later."

"I will . . . promise."

Sophie nodded. "'Kay, gotta dash." She took off down the hall, her hair swinging wildly around her. I smiled. I'd tell her about Ash, but maybe I could finally tell her my bigger secret.

A locker slammed shut near my head, and Glen's sneering face appeared. Miranda stood close to his side, smirking.

"Lila, it looks like you have a teensy crush on Ash," she said with mock sincerity. "That's so cute, but . . . don't you think he's just a little out of your league? No offense or anything."

I glared at both of them, vacillating between anger and humiliation. *Don't you think you're a wench? No offense or anything.* Without a word, I turned and walked down the hall toward my locker.

Glen's voice carried through the air behind her. "I thought you could speak, you little freak."

I wanted to tell him that Dr. Seuss had nothing on him, but instead, I did what I always did and stayed silent. It was the safer route—best not to call extra attention to myself. Their idiotic comments were an expected part of my day, yet mentioning Ash somehow hurt more than usual. I tried to focus on the positive. A nice boy was waiting for me in English class. This thought propelled me to walk even faster to grab my textbook and get to class. In less than two minutes I'd see those cute green eyes again.

I dialed my combination in record time and flung open my locker. My heart stopped and the chemistry book fell from my hands. Taped to the inside of the door was a picture.

I stared at the photo in horror, not quite believing what I saw. The bloody faerie wings from the news stared back at me in vivid, nauseating color—and scrawled across the picture in red ink were two words: *You're next.*

SECRET SANTA

The One is growing in strength, which forces me to rattle them a bit. I leave photo gifts for several of the freaks at various schools within close proximity of each other. By gauging their reactions, I can narrow down my list. In truth, it is also partly for my own enjoyment, but you can tell a lot about someone by the way they react under stress. Maybe their response will give me a clue as to whether they are the garden variety kind versus the One. It isn't cruel; it's simply basic psychology.

I whittle down the list of possible names, several of them at the same school. One runs crying down the hall soon after finding my present. It makes me smile. Maybe my offering is morbid, but it can't be said that I'm not a giver. It is only a shame that what I give, I must also take away.

No. It isn't a shame. I can't wait to take it.

DEADBEAT FATHERS

S taring at the picture, a part of me wanted to run as fast as possible out of the school to the safety of home. Yet the math-oriented, analytical part of my brain kicked in and urged me to continue with my day as usual. I reasoned that a) leaving school would draw even more attention to me, and b) walking home alone with a killer nearby wouldn't make me the sharpest knife in the drawer, so I reached conclusion c) staying at school was the safest option. However, I was shaking so hard I didn't know how acting normal would be possible.

I forced myself to walk to the next class, my shoes feeling like lead weights. *Don't think about bloody wings; think happy thoughts.* I imagined the soothing sounds of the surf pounding against the shore, and relaxed a little, only to have memories of my dream crash back into me. Now my head was filled with nothing but images of dismembered faeries.

I was vaguely aware of a girl running past me in tears but didn't look up in time to see who it was. By the time I reached class, the shaking had subsided to mild tremors. Maybe I could claim a caffeine overload.

Ash waited at the door and looked me over from head to toe. "What's wrong?" he asked.

Nothing much, just a nervous breakdown. "I don't feel well." As I fought to stay calm, Ash grasped my arm in an attempt to steady me. Unfortunately, his touch made my heart race —and my wings. I tried to ignore them, but my back blazed with pain.

I snatched my arm away. "Sorry, it's not you." I raced to my seat in the front row.

He called after me from his back-row seat, "Let's grab lunch after class."

I cringed, knowing my classmates were eating up this exchange. I managed a weak smile over my shoulder. "Sure."

Mr. Finch lectured about the thematic elements found in *A Midsummer Night's Dream*. I couldn't help thinking that it would be easier to be one of Shakespeare's fictional faeries. At least there weren't any heinous faerie-killers in his stories.

My mind drifted back to the picture from my locker, which was now crumpled in the bottom of my backpack. My lock hadn't been damaged, so how did someone get in there? More importantly, *who* got in there? Did they know I was a faerie or only suspect it? Maybe I'd said too much in chem class, or maybe someone just wanted to scare me— someone who'd run out of jabs about my clothes and needed new material.

I was so absorbed in my thoughts that the class flew by. For once, I wished I wasn't in the front row; I couldn't seem to focus like usual. I snapped back to attention at the very end when Mr. Finch gave us an essay assignment on Shakespeare that was due Friday. He stood in front of his desk and leaned back against it with his arms crossed, peering at all of us. "That gives you only two nights to work on it. Please know that I expect great essays, as you've shown tremendous talent so far and have set the bar high for yourselves."

Several kids groaned as they trudged out the door. I shoved my book into my backpack and stood, at the same time that Mr. Finch stepped away from his desk. A pencil at the edge of his desk rolled off and landed at my feet.

He put a hand up and smiled when I moved to get it. "I've got it."

He leaned over and scooped it up quickly—but not before I saw. The hairs on the back of my neck stood up.

When he bent over in front of me, the shirt collar at the back of his neck underneath his blazer gaped open slightly, and for a split second, I saw the unmistakable edging of binding material.

Mr. Finch stood and smiled. "Lila, you are one of my best students, so I hope to have a fantastic essay from you Friday."

I hoped the shock didn't register on my face. "I'll . . . I'll do my best."

He tilted his head at me. "Is everything okay?"

Aside from the fact that you have wings? "Yes, just hungry, I think. Bye, Mr. Finch." I'd wondered if there were other faerie students at Northeast, but I'd never considered that there could be a faerie teacher. How many of us were there?

Ash waited just outside the classroom door. "Hey, quiet girl, you feeling any better?"

No. Someone wants to kill me, and I just discovered Mr. Finch is a faerie. "Um, a little, I guess." We headed to the cafeteria, my head still spinning.

"This probably isn't the time to tell you that I heard the lunch choices today are meat loaf and corn dogs." He raised one eyebrow in mock concern. "Your mints may come in handy again."

"Gross," I said. "Guess I'll do my old standby of Fritos and Diet Coke."

Ash laughed. "The lunch of champions. I brought lunch today if you want to share."

Sophie passed by on my right side as we reached the cafeteria entrance. "Hey, wanna skip the meat loaf surprise and go out for burritos?" She nodded at Ash. "You can come too."

Burritos were normally one of my favorite things, but I knew I couldn't eat a bite. I shook my head. "Not today, Soph."

"Suit yourself. Have fun, kids." She winked at me, like I had declined the offer because I wanted to have some time alone with Ash, then jetted to find someone else for her burrito excursion.

Ash sat across from me and fished a sandwich out of his backpack. Despite still being freaked out about the picture in my locker, I tried to concentrate on what he was saying— something about being from Asheville, North Carolina, originally but living the past few years in Philadelphia, until his mom decided to move back to warmer weather.

He held out his other sandwich half to me. "Want it?"

I shook my head. "No thanks." My skin prickled, and I turned to find Glen scowling at me from across the cafeteria. Geez, it wasn't like I was the only nerd in school; he could easily find someone else to torture.

"How do you like Chapel Hill so far?" I asked, turning back to Ash.

"I've visited before, when I lived in Asheville, and really liked the vibe. My mom loves it; she wants me to go to college here. My sister, well, half-sister, Corrine, goes to college up in Philly—she's a junior and didn't want to move. But we still talk all the time."

I sighed. "That's great. Being an only child is kind of a drag sometimes. What about your dad?"

"Long story," he said simply, and took a bite of his sandwich. "But I'll tell you another time."

This was officially the longest conversation I'd ever had with a boy, and I liked it. Which of course meant it was the perfect time for Miranda and Lexie to saunter past with their lunch trays. Lexie bobbled her tray, and her orange rolled off onto the floor near Ash's shoe. He leaned over to pick it up for her, but Lexie was faster. She bent forward at the same time he did, pushing her ample chest toward his face. She wore a glittery spaghetti-strap tank top that barely covered her. Their hands touched the orange at the same time, and Lexie lingered a few seconds longer than necessary, making sure he got an eyeful.

"Sorry," she giggled. "Thanks Ash, you're a sweetheart."

And you're so not following school dress code.

As she and Miranda walked away, Lexie called over her shoulder, "By the way, my parents are out of town this weekend and I'm having a little get-together, if you want to come."

Ash glanced at her, then back at me. "Thanks, I appreciate the invite, but I have plans with Lila this weekend."

I almost spit out my Diet Coke. Both Miranda and Lexie looked stunned.

"Well, of course you can bring her—if you want," said Lexie. She glared at me, flipped her hair over her shoulder and marched to the door.

"Sorry," said Ash, "but that's one get-together I don't want any part of."

"Don't be sorry." I processed his words: *I have plans with Lila this weekend.*

Ash put his hand on top of mine. "Wow, you have really soft hands. I bet you hear that all the time."

My heart skipped a beat. Part of it was that Ash was touching me, but most of it was *what* he'd said.

I remembered Mom holding my hand when I was young. "Ah, you have the hands of a faerie for sure," she had told me. "No human has hands quite as soft."

Ash stroked the back of my hand with his thumb. My wings went nuts under the bindings, but I couldn't tear my hand away. "Thanks. And no, I haven't really heard that much." *Because the number of boys' hands I've held can now be counted on one finger.*

He smiled. "I was serious about this weekend, you know. Do you want to catch a movie or something?"

Or something. I was shocked the moment I thought it. I was the girl who always had her homework finished, was always early for class. I was the responsible one. Wanting to kiss this boy was so not responsible. *Get a grip on yourself, Lila.* My wings continued to punish me, so I focused on the fact that seeing him would not be an option. It would have been iffy even before the news last night, but now I knew Mom wouldn't let me out of her sight. I wouldn't be seeing a movie with Ash, or with Sophie. It was a miracle she'd even let me come to school today.

"Ah, love: the sweet salve on the harshness of humanity."

I looked up in embarrassment. "Hey, Curtis."

Curtis bowed. "Hello, maiden. Hav'st thee decided on thy essay for literature?"

Ash's brow furrowed.

"Not yet. You?"

"No. I will give it some thought and figure it out by the morrow. Fare thee well." He tipped his imaginary cap and moved on through the loud cafeteria.

Ash looked at me. "Who? What?"

I laughed. "That's Curtis. He's . . . different. I heard he works at the Renaissance festival in the summer, and does like, Civil War re-enactments or something."

"Interesting. To each his own." He finished the last bite of his sandwich. "So, what about this weekend?"

I sighed. "I can't this weekend. It's just that, well, my mom is really strict."

"I could drive you home from school today?"

I gulped. "Not a good idea."

"Why?"

Where to start? "My mom would freak if she saw a strange boy drive me up to the house. She's a tad overprotective."

"So maybe I could come to your house tonight—after you convince her I'm not strange?" He raised an eyebrow at me. "Just to work on our English paper, of course . . . it *is* due Friday. Then maybe we can figure out this weekend."

Maybe. If I wasn't allowed to leave the house, maybe I could convince her to let someone visit. "I'll ask."

Ash grinned. "Great, then I need your number so I can call you later."

I tried to act casual, as if giving out my number was something I did every day. I wasn't about to tell him that I'd never talked to a boy on the phone before. But that was about to change. Now Ash Cooper had my number.

The rest of the day went by in a blur. Even when Glen bumped into me, and my books fell everywhere, I took it in stride. It seemed to piss him off even more when I showed no reaction to his Neanderthal antics, his rage escalating when Curtis stopped to help me pick them up and called me "milady" in front of him. I thanked him by tipping an imaginary cap his way. He smiled as he took his leave.

Hallway chatter about the sensational news story seemed never ending. Ms. Rouelle began French class by saying she didn't want to hear another word about faeries as she was *très fatigué* of the topic. Fear trickled down my spine whenever I thought about the picture, so conjugating French verbs served as a welcome, albeit temporary, distraction.

I walked home with Sophie, checking behind me every few minutes as if a killer might jump out from behind the trees like they did in horror movies.

"What is your deal?" Sophie asked, turning around to look behind us. "It's like you're expecting someone." Her eyes grew wide and she squealed. "Wait, is it Ash? Is he coming over to your house?"

"Of course not; don't be silly." I forced myself to focus on the ground in front of us. "I'm fine."

I wasn't fine at all. Between fear of being killed and fear about Mom's reaction to Ash coming over, I was a giant ball of stress. I couldn't, under any circumstances, show her the photo from my locker. It would be the end of my brief stint at an actual school, and she'd probably move us across the country.

We'd had countless discussions in which Mom had extolled the virtues of continued homeschooling. She'd only relented after enduring months of my tearful pleas. She'd love an excuse to keep me contained in the home at all times. Keeping my identity hidden was isolating enough, and though I was hardly a social butterfly, I couldn't bear the thought of being so lonely again. There was no choice but to keep the photo a secret, at least for now.

Sophie sighed. "Okay, I don't believe you, but we're still on for the movies Saturday, right? Unless you're blowing me off for that hottie . . . not that I'd blame you."

I walked next to her, ignoring the urge to look over my shoulder again and make sure we weren't being followed. "Well, maybe. It's just that—"

"No way! You are blowing me off for him."

I shook my head. "No, no, that's not it. I just sense I might be grounded or something."

Sophie laughed. "Ha, that's a good one. You've never been in trouble, like, ever."

I sighed. I'd have to deal with that this weekend. Having a good reputation made it hard to get out of things without lying.

We walked along in silence for a few minutes, which allowed me to listen for footsteps following behind us. Luckily, the only sound was the whir of Curtis's skateboard as he blew past us and waved. I waved back, and turned to Sophie as we reached her street. "I promise that I will try to be at that bloodbath movie with you this weekend . . . I'll do my best."

Sophie rolled her eyes. "Of course you'll be there. Don't be so dramatic." She hitched her backpack over her shoulder. "I'll text you later. We *have* to study tonight. The chem test is in two days!"

"'Kay, see ya, Soph."

I watched her stroll down the block, and wondered how it felt to be so carefree.

I walked up the sidewalk to our house, noticing the color-coordinated flowers adorning the path and the perfectly trimmed shrubs lining the front yard. Mom spent hours out there, making sure everything was meticulous. A lone dandelion would be yanked out immediately, the sanctity of her work somehow threatened by a wayward weed.

"Hi, Mrs. Nesbaum." I waved to nosy Nellie, who was

tending her roses near the neighboring gate with a pair of shears.

"What was that, dear?" She turned, squinting in my direction.

"I was just saying hello," I called louder.

"Oh, hello there—and give your mother my regards as well." Mrs. Nesbaum winked at me before she resumed pruning the deadheads from the fragrant bushes.

Mom practically ran to the door when I walked in. "You're home! How was it today, sweetie? I made you cookies."

I marched straight past her in response and dropped my backpack on the floor. I flopped down into one of the refinished chairs, feeling like the lemon-yellow shade on the kitchen walls was trying a bit too hard. The flowered fabric on the chairs seemed too bright, like forced cheerfulness. Mom's décor choices agitated me today.

"Mom, we have to talk." I wasn't going to let her off the hook this time.

She frowned for a second but recovered quickly. She smiled while setting a plate of cookies on the table.

"Of course, sweetie. What is it?" She pushed the plate toward me and sat down at the opposite end of the small wooden table.

I shoved the plate away. "I know what happened. All the kids at school were talking about it today. Did you really think I wouldn't find out that a faerie was murdered?"

Mom's face crumpled. "I'm so sorry. I didn't want you to hear those awful things. My baby . . ." She reached her arm across the table to take my hand.

"I'm not a baby anymore, Mom." I pulled my arm back. "You can't protect me by pretending it isn't happening. Someone out there is killing faeries—"

"We don't know that," Mom interjected. "it was only one faerie they talked about on the news, and—"

"Oh, come on Mom, there are only a few thousand of my kind left. 'Only one faerie' is a big deal to me." I cringed, thinking of the picture from my locker. Plus, I couldn't explain it—maybe part of it was the nightmare I'd had—but I knew in my gut that it wasn't just one faerie killing.

Mom sighed. "I thought it would only worry you, and trust me, I worry more than enough for both of us. I'm just trying to give you the normal childhood you deserve."

I scoffed. "I'm not normal, so there's no use trying to pretend I am. I'm not six years old anymore. I deserve to know."

Nodding, Mom sank back in her chair. "You're right. I should have told you. I didn't want to scare you. Up until last night, all I ever worried about was that you might be bullied. I never imagined anyone would want you dead." Tears welled up in her eyes.

I didn't blink. "There's something else I need to know. You've never told me anything about my father—my biological father, I mean. He was a faerie after all, so maybe there are some super-secret faerie survival tips I've missed out on."

She looked down at the table. "I don't have much to say."

I couldn't contain my irritation another second and slammed my hand onto the table. She jumped. "You never have much to say about him! I don't know *anything* about him, aside from the fact that you cheated on your husband with him."

Mom looked shocked. "Don't you dare speak to me like that!"

I couldn't stop the tears leaking from my eyes as I shouted. "Do you how hard it is to not know anyone else who's like me? Maybe my father has answers for me. Maybe he knows something that can help me." I took a breath and wiped a tear from my face. I reached out for her hand. "Please, Mom, I need to know."

Mom clasped my hand in hers. "I know. I . . . I would tell you if I knew, but I don't know where he is. I haven't for a long time."

Sniffling, I stared at her. "How could you not know?"

She squeezed my hand tighter. "It happened several weeks before you were born. I haven't seen or heard from him since. He . . . disappeared."

Looking into Mom's eyes, I couldn't be sure if she was holding something back—her specialty. "Disappeared how?"

"He left without a trace. No note, nothing. I don't know what else to say, Lila." She looked as if she might say more, but didn't.

"How about what he was like? His favorite food? What type of music did he listen to? You have to give me something here."

Tears leaked out of Mom's eyes as she shook her head slowly.

"Seriously? Wow, Mom. I don't even want to be around you right now." I stormed down the hall and slammed the door to my room. There was so much to process, and I felt so crappy that I wasn't sure I even wanted to try to have Ash over later. It's not like I could ever have a real relationship anyway. My secret would have to come out sooner or later.

I lay in my bed, reeling with emotion and exhaustion. I thought I'd rest until I calmed down; however, within minutes of my head hitting the pillow, a fitful sleep overcame me. I fell into the same terrifying dream . . . almost.

Faeries were dying all around me, their dismembered

wings strewn about the shoreline. I knew I would be next as the sun sank into the sea. Only one thing was different. A male faerie flew near me. Though I didn't know him, he was strangely familiar to me. I could barely hear him as he whispered in my ear—he told me to fly as fast as I could. I begged him to come with me, but he said that he couldn't. He said that he was already dead.

CHATTY CATHY

M y assessment of the majority of people online? Unbelievably stupid. They don't realize how much information they share about themselves, especially in their inane status updates and tweets. Once you get them in a chat room they'll tell you anything. More importantly, they'll believe anything you spoonfeed them.

I type I'm quite interested in visiting you to discuss this in person. I barely hit Send, when beyhive4eva98 responds with definitely. It is almost too easy. If I am right—and I usually am —this one is a faerophile and will lead me to multiple faeries. Granted, I'll have to take a minor detour to see her, but I'm guessing she will prove quite useful in my mission.

STUDY SESSION

ictures of dead faeries and Ash melded together in a weird mash-up as I woke from my nap. *Ash.* I definitely wanted him to come over. Knowing how much Mom regretted keeping the news from me, I played the guilt card. Not only played it, but milked it for all it was worth, which is how one Ash Cooper ended up at my house Wednesday night. I texted Sophie that I couldn't talk tonight and would catch up with her at school the next day.

When he got here, I could tell from Mom's eyes that she was terrified, that she thought it was a huge risk to bring an outsider into our home. However, within a few minutes, I noticed a slight, almost involuntary smile as she spoke to him. She excused herself after a few more minutes, leaving me completely alone with him on the living room couch.

Surrounded by books, we discussed Shakespeare's play. Ash propped up his feet on the coffee table and leaned back against the couch, his hands cupped behind his head. The haphazard way he flung his jacket over the side of the couch bothered me, but I resisted the compulsion to place it neatly on a hanger. It was progress.

"So, which theme are you going to write about?" he asked. "The absurdity of love? The magic represented by the faeries?"

I thought about the story. "No, I think I'll write about dreams and the impact of dreaming on our waking selves."

"Whoa, pretty deep there, Lila." He smiled. "Four days will quickly steep themselves in night. . . .'"

I smiled shyly. "'Four nights will quickly dream away the time,'" I finished.

He arched one eyebrow. "Well done."

"Thanks. So what about you?" I asked.

"Me? I'm going with the faeries—I like a little magic and mystery. Plus, in those pictures in the book, they're pretty cute."

My heart hammered. *He thinks faeries are cute. Maybe there is hope for us.* I shook my head, trying to clear the thought. Instead I asked him, "Did you hear all the stuff people were saying about the faerie murder on the news?"

"Yeah," said Ash. His brow furrowed. "I saw it on TV. Some stupid sicko out there trying to scare people. It pisses me off that someone would destroy a creature so rare. Let's talk about something else."

Surprised by his anger, I reached over to grab one of the textbooks from the table to change the topic back to school-work. My hair brushed his arm, and the look on his face changed.

"You have beautiful hair, you know." He reached up and twirled one of my wavy locks around his finger. "It's almost as soft as your hands."

Torn between sheer terror about where this could lead and loving the feel of his touch, I leaned slightly toward him. "It's kind of impossible to focus on the thematic elements of Shakespeare when you're doing that."

His finger lingered a moment longer, and then he let go of my hair. "Sorry."

A cough startled me. "Just me, forgot my milk." Mom walked into the kitchen behind us and I straightened up on the couch, opening my textbook.

Mom's appearance had helped me regain my senses— somewhat. What was I thinking? It's not like I could let him touch me. If he even so much as rubbed my back, he'd feel the bindings underneath my pathetic excuse for a shirt.

I opened my book. "We should probably get to work."

Ash frowned. "Fine, but you can't stop me from looking at you while we work."

No boy had been interested in me before, and I flushed in embarrassment and stared at my book.

Ash leaned close again. Close enough for my wings to quicken. He had his book in hand, and a smile on his lips. "Okay, where were we? Ah yes, the impact of dreams . . ."

The more we discussed the assignment, the more I liked him. Ash surprised me with his belief in magic and his openness to the unknown. Maybe he wouldn't be disgusted to find out I was one of the characters we were talking about. Except that the only similarity I had to those faeries were my wings. I wished I possessed the magic they did.

I was writing notes in the margin of my book when Mom reappeared. She smiled at us before yawning. "Sweetie, it's late and you need your sleep. I'm sure Ash needs to be getting home too."

"Wow, I lost track of the time. Sorry, Ms. Kincade." Ash jammed his book into his backpack and smiled at Mom. "Thanks again for having me over."

"You're welcome here anytime, Ash. That is, anytime before midnight." She turned to me. "I expect you to be in bed in five minutes."

A rush of excitement flooded through me. She'd said that Ash was allowed to come back.

"You hear that?" asked Ash after Mom had retreated down the hallway. "You're stuck with me, Lila Kincade. I'm coming back—your mom said so."

"I guess you're coming back, then," I said with mock seriousness, "so we can work more on our assignment." I walked him to the door.

"Riiiiight, our assignment. Since it's due on Friday, guess I'll be back tomorrow."

I cracked a smile. "Fine, tomorrow night then. Don't forget your books."

"I've been thinking about your topic—the whole effect of dreaming on your waking life thing. Maybe we should test whether the opposite is true—whether your waking life impacts your dreaming." With that, he tipped up my chin and kissed me lightly on the lips before stepping away. It lasted mere seconds, yet I was stunned. *I finally found something I like better than algebra.*

"Night, Lila. I want to hear all about your dreams tomorrow—and I really hope that I impact them." He gave me a devilish grin and walked out the door.

All I managed to call after him was, "Night."

"So, he seems nice, Lila. Do you like him?" Mom was unbinding my wings before bed, which felt amazing as they'd been bound since first thing that morning. The last thing I wanted to do was talk about was my feelings for Ash. I'd rather just go to sleep and dream about him—and that short-but-sweet kiss.

"Um, he's okay," I said, and yawned loudly, trying to give her the hint.

Mom unwound the mesh fabric as I faced away from her. "Look sweetie, I want you to be happy. I also want you to be safe, okay?"

I jerked my head around in disbelief. "*Safe?* Are you talking about birth control?"

"Oh, goodness . . . no." She looked distraught. "I just meant safe about your wings."

I heaved a sigh of relief. "No worries there, Mom. We're just friends."

Mom stood, smoothing down her shirt. "Well, I know that friendships can turn into something more. I hope you know you can always talk to me about anything. I was young once too, you know." She pulled a greenish-colored crystal from her pocket and placed it on the stand next to my bed. I didn't want to know what it was for.

"Sure, Mom. Night." I pulled the covers up and turned over on my side, yawning.

She sighed and switched off the light. "Night."

Lying in bed, I fantasized about Ash coming over on a Sunday, my favorite day of the week. I could stay unbound all day, though only in the house. Of course, that would mean he'd know I was a faerie, which couldn't happen, but a girl could dream.

Even being unbound wasn't always enough for me. It was better than the alternative, but I still wished I were free to fly. I already knew how that request would go over.

I'd been five years old. After finishing one of Mom's homeschooling lessons, I took a ruler and wiggled it under my shirt, wedging it between my wings and the fabric binding. I jiggled the ruler back and forth, back and forth, until the binding loosened and the tape came off. I gripped the loose fabric and unwound it from my wings. Then I flew above the bed, following the trail of flowers on the border near my ceiling. I peeked out the open window, and the fresh air summoned me right out of it. I flew out the window and into the trees in the backyard.

I hadn't known the feeling of a fresh breeze against my wings until that wondrous day in the backyard—I dipped and flew among the tree branches without a care in the world. Mom happened to be scrubbing dishes in the kitchen at the time. When she saw me through the kitchen window, she screamed, dashing outside. "Lila, get down here this instant!"

I hovered in the air by a bird's nest, wanting so much to obey her, yet craving a few more minutes of freedom. My lips in a full pout, I lowered slowly to the ground. "I never get to have any fun."

Old Mrs. Nesbaum had appeared by the back fence. "Is everything all right over here? I heard a scream."

"Everything is fine, Mrs. Nesbaum. I thought Lila got hurt, but she's okay." Mom motioned for me to scoot in the house.

"What was that, dearie? Lila got in the dirt?"

"Lila is fine, Mrs. Nesbaum. She's just fine!" She turned to me. "Missy, you are in trouble. Now get to your room."

She hadn't understood that flying was so much more fun than walking. What good were wings if you couldn't use them? That was eleven years ago, and I hadn't flown since. Now I had to be content with simply having my wings unbound. Even when I was alone in my room, I didn't so much as lift an inch off the ground. I didn't trust myself. If I got even a hint of breeze in my lifted wings, I'd be too tempted. I might fly out the window and try to touch the moon, the stars. I might never come back.

12

DEATH AND HIKING

L ucky me. *Beyhive4eva98 turns out to be a gold mine.
She is indeed a faerophile and unwittingly provides me
with a wealth of information. It will cause her great
sadness to know what I do with that information, but I need even
more from her, so I'll keep her around . . . for now.*

*There they are—a small group of freaks enjoying an outing
in the late-afternoon woods. I am ready. They chat and laugh,
stumbling on the occasional tree root. They have no clue how
vulnerable they are. Their human façades don't fool me for a
minute.*

*The One isn't with them. I feel it. Yet I also feel the One's
surge in strength. I'll have to take him or her out before they can
use their newfound powers. I can't let them wreck all the good I
want to accomplish. I might be cruel, but my intentions are noble.*

*After all, this is war. Killing others in the name of war is
accepted practice—how could we learn anything different from
history? I look back at the group: Two hold hands. I spit on the
ground. Love isn't something those freaks deserve. Anger rages
through me, but I have a job to do. The sun begins to sink in the
sky and I know it is almost time.*

I am outnumbered, but that does not concern me. I am faster. I survey the group heading toward me and finger my trusty blade.

It looks like I might actually have to exert myself this time. I smile.

13

WARDROBE MALFUNCTION

A t school, I'd promised Sophie I'd find a way to go to the movies with her on Saturday, and would fill her in on everything then. In between classes, I'd whispered to her that Ash had come over last night. She'd hugged me and said "I'm so proud of you," like I'd just gotten into MIT. Mom might let me go to me the movies if both Sophie and Ash went with me. There was safety in numbers, plus I wanted my best friend and . . . whatever Ash was turning out to be . . . to get along.

True to her word, Mom let Ash come over again after school. But she made it clear he had to leave by nine o'clock. I didn't care. In fact, I was borderline ecstatic. Since our essays were due the next day, we talked for a while, then spent a chunk of time typing away side by side on our laptops. The quick clicking of our keys in unison was comforting, and we had an easy, comfortable silence while we worked. I finished my essay and looked over at Ash. He looked deep in thought as his fingers flew over the keyboard. Streaks of light from the setting sun shone through the window, and I stared out, imagining what it would be like to fly through the pink and orange swirls.

A sudden twinge made me sit up straighter. *It almost feels like it did when*—sickness slammed into me, and I ran to the bathroom, making it just in time to vomit the remains of my dinner. Could I have some sort of rare faerie disease only known about back in our realm? I'd consider making a doctor's appointment, but knew the examination gown would expose more than my butt.

I washed my face and rinsed out my mouth, waiting for the feeling to pass. The queasiness finally faded and I felt somewhat normal, except for a sense of exhaustion. I patted my face with a hand towel and went back to the couch.

I grabbed one of the mints from my backpack and popped it in my mouth, hoping it would cover the puke smell. These mints were the reason I'd met Ash in the first place. It was strange something that small could bring two people together.

"Everything okay?" Ash had stopped typing and was staring intently at me.

I tried to act nonchalant. "Yeah, I'm fine." I gestured at his computer. "How's it going?"

"Good. Almost finished—you're faster with your hands I guess," he said. He went back to pecking at the keys in front of him. I couldn't help but notice how his muscles flexed as he typed.

Ash looked up from his computer again and grinned when he caught me staring.

"See something you like?" he asked.

My cheeks burned. "I think you like making me blush."

"You do look even cuter with pink in your cheeks," he teased, and took my hand in his. "How long do we have before your mom kicks me out?"

"Probably another hour." I sighed. "The time goes by really fast when you're here."

"Well, I'm not about to waste an hour," he said. He took his palm and placed it over mine, then ran his hand lightly up my arm. His hand reached my face and he traced the outline of my lips with his thumb. "Even your lips are crazy soft."

I really hoped I didn't smell like vomit. I also wished I'd had more practice kissing, but I had never seen online tutorials on making out like I had for math. Ash grasped the bottom of my shirt and tugged me toward him. Our lips inched closer together, so close now, and his hands moved to my waist. What if I didn't kiss right? A mix of terror and desire fought inside me. My back was on fire, my wings relentless in their beating against the bindings.

A small tearing sound broke the silence of the room.

Ash jerked his head back. "What was that?"

I froze. *Oh no, not now.* For the first time ever, one of my wings had succeeded in tearing the tape that held the fabric over them. The binding material slipped down over the tip of my wing. He had to go. Now.

"Um, nothing. I think my shirt might've ripped a little." I leaned back against the couch, pressing my wayward wing against a firmer surface. "You should probably go now—my mom will be out here soon."

"Just like that? What's wrong, Lila?"

I shook my head, afraid to speak—afraid to move.

"Did I move too fast?"

"No, it has nothing to do with you. I like you . . . I just need a little time." *And a little tape.*

"Okay." Ash sighed and stood. "Walk me out?" He took my hand and attempted to pull me toward him. If I leaned away from the couch, my right wing might spring open. I snatched my hand away from him. It was the only way to get him to leave.

"Just go."

Ash looked confused.

My wing attempted to beat its way out of my shirt. "Now!"

His look of bewilderment turned to hurt, then anger. He gathered his laptop and books, shoving them into his bag. He slung the bag over his back and stomped to the door. My heart screamed at me to stop him—to explain everything, but my head knew that wasn't an option. My head won; I remained silent. Ash hesitated at the door a moment, as if hoping I would say something. I didn't. He opened the door and walked out into the night. He didn't look back.

14

CURIOUSER AND CURIOUSER

My frustration grows as my patience diminishes. There are more of these aberrant beings than I first imagined. Sadly, Chapel Hill isn't the only high-density area; I've already made my way through England and was positive that I would find the One there. For once, I was wrong—though I did manage to take out a good number of garden-variety freaks. Now I must slog through this humid southern cesspool. No matter.

It will be worth it; the One has to be here. I know it. But for all the killing I've done, I still feel so far from my goal. Curious that I haven't found the One yet. And worse, several on my list of possibilities no longer seem to belong there. One didn't react at all to my gift. For all my steps forward, I feel like I am losing ground.

The recurring dream has started to fray at my nerves a bit. It is always the same—I relish in killing them all and feel unstoppable. All except one, who remains just out of my reach. That one refuses to die. I know what I have to do. Time to pick up the pace.

15

THE TIES THAT BIND

Friday started out badly and took a nosedive from there. Ash didn't speak to me—at all. In fact, during AA, he seemed to speak to everyone *but* me. While I withdrew further into my shell, his loud laughter reverberated throughout the room. With the threat of murder hanging over me, it seemed ridiculous to let Ash's silent treatment bother me so much, but he was, after all, my first crush.

Worse, I was ill. My stomach was a train wreck. I'd barely made it to the bathroom in time, only to find someone had scratched a new message in the stall: *The only good faerie is a dead one.* Lovely. The murder had empowered the faerie racists to speak their minds. This time, the nausea lingered all morning; it didn't disappear the way it had before.

In chem class, I said hi to Jacinda, but otherwise kept silent. From his desk, Mr. Birchester looked at me strangely several times. He asked me to stay after class. *Maybe going back to homeschooling wasn't such a terrible idea after all.*

"Lila, you've gone from being uncharacteristically chatty

back to the church mouse I know. Is there anything you'd like to talk about?" he asked.

I shook my head quickly, afraid that if I opened my mouth, I'd cry. Before he could say anything else, I turned and ran out the door. Barely aware of my surroundings, I'd almost reached my locker when I saw Lexie at the end locker on the corner. Just when I thought things couldn't get any worse. She giggled at something the person around the corner said to her. My stomach dropped. I knew the voice.

Of all places, Ash had chosen here to flirt with the person who was widely considered to be one of the most virginally challenged people in the whole school, second only to a linebacker on the football team. *You've got to be kidding me.*

Lexie broke off mid-giggle and glared at me. Once again, I'd said something out loud that I had meant to keep silent. She turned back to Ash. "C'mon, I want to hear the rest of that story. You're hilarious." Lexie tugged on his shirt for him to follow her as they walked past me. Ash hesitated by the locker, turning to meet my eyes.

I flung open my locker, almost smacking him in the face.

"Whatever," he muttered, and turned to follow Lexie.

"Looks like Ash has moved on to greener pastures." I turned around to see Miranda sneering at me, Glen at her side. Miranda flashed a sarcastic look of sympathy. "I guess you thought you were pretty special for a minute there?"

Glen laughed. "More like special-ed. Guess he realized what a freak you are."

"Shut up, you obnoxious moron." I couldn't believe I'd spoken back to him for once, and he must not have believed it either, because he was momentarily speechless. But not for long.

He strode up to me and raised his hand to my chin,

lifting it up. Anyone walking by would think it was an intimate gesture, almost romantic. I pressed myself back against my locker. Glen pressed his fingers into my cheek, squeezing. He spoke softly. "Don't you know freaks should be seen and not heard? It would be a shame if anything happened to this pretty face." He squeezed harder. "I'd watch my back if I were you."

Miranda's smirk faded and her eyes widened. "Glen, come on. Let's go." She pulled him away from me, tugging him down the hallway.

I trembled long after they had disappeared. *Freak? Watch my back?* Did he suspect I had wings there? I pulled my English textbook and folder from my locker, trying to ignore the sick feeling in my stomach. It had been stupid to think I could ever fit in at a regular school.

And why did I think I could ever have a boyfriend like a normal person? Still, Ash could have waited more than five seconds before moving on. To add insult to injury, Ash and I now had the same class, where we'd be presenting the assignments we'd worked on together. At least Lexie wasn't in that class—she'd have to wield her breasts on another unsuspecting male for the next hour.

Ash sat sideways in his seat, talking to several guys near him about the football game that weekend.

"There's no way we're going down to those losers," one guy said.

Ash nodded in agreement. "Yeah, their quarterback is good, but he's no match for our defensive ends. We'll kick ass for sure."

He's acting like he's gone to Northeast longer than a week. I walked by them, trying not to shake, and sank into my seat. Luckily, Mr. Finch started class right on time. Several students in succession went to the front of the room to discuss their assignment from *A Midsummer Night's Dream*. That night with Ash started to feel like it had been just a dream. How did I go from having my first kiss to this misery within days? I paid scarce attention to my classmates—until Ash was called to the front of the room.

"My chosen thematic element from the story is magic," he began. "In Shakespeare's play, this magic was represented by the faeries. They served as a mechanism to propel the action forward . . ." Ash continued with his essay, looking at the paper in his hand.

He didn't include anything we had discussed at my house. Nothing about the wonder of magic and alternative realities. He didn't even mention the faeries' cuteness factor. Ash looked up from his paper and stared right at me. "In the end, I thought their only real purpose was to reveal the absurd nature of humans. To remind us that nothing is as it seems."

I shifted in my seat.

"Interesting interpretation, Ashton," said Mr. Finch. "I cannot wait to read more from you. You may take your seat. Lila, you are last but not least."

I walked to the front of the class and stood there, surveying the room. I gripped my paper, preparing to give a short summary about the importance of dreams in the play. Dreams. Dreams of dead faeries filled my head. Dreams of Ash kissing me and walking away. Looking out at the class, I saw a sea of clueless faces. They didn't care about the impact of dreaming on waking life. My eyes fell on Ash. There was no way I could speak of dreams while in the midst of a waking nightmare.

I handled it really well: I burst into tears. I mumbled an apology to Mr. Finch, handed him my paper, and ran from class. Rather than face the cafeteria next period, where Ash would likely be with Lexie, I found an empty classroom where I sat alone, sobbing. The only positive spin I could put on things was that my wings had been quiet all day. *Note to self: Nothing keeps wings in check like a healthy dose of depression.*

The bell rang. I had to pull myself together if I was going to make it to French class. At least Ash wasn't in there. If only out of sight meant out of mind. I walked toward my locker, my hair covering most of my face.

"There you are, Lila. I've been searching for you. Are you well?" Mr. Finch asked, concern furrowing his brow. His glasses slipped, and he pushed the wire frames up his long, thin nose.

I thought of his bound wings beneath his shirt and wished I could tell him I knew how it felt. "Yes, I'm fine. Stage fright, I guess. I'm sorry. It won't happen again." I hoped my eyes weren't as swollen as they felt.

"Are you sure that's all?" Mr. Finch smiled. "It seems like there may be a little boy trouble going on. I noticed a sudden . . . distance, shall we say . . . from a certain gentleman?"

I nodded. "Yes, but I'll be okay."

He nodded. "Okay. I'm here if you need to talk."

"Thanks, Mr. Finch." I walked away and took a deep breath before rounding the corner to my locker. It was clear. Not a green-eyed boy in sight. All I could think of was getting home and holing up in my room until morning. Maybe I'd pretend to be sick tomorrow. Maybe I wouldn't come back at all. Mom would jump at the chance to home-school me again.

Before the locker opened all the way, a picture fell out. It floated to the ground and landed at my feet. I picked it up and stared at it, not quite comprehending at first. Lavender wings covered in blood. Disembodied and lifeless. I hadn't heard about another murder, but these were, without a doubt, the wings of a very deceased faerie. I tried to ignore the analytical part of my mind screaming that this meant the killer had been in the school, or still was, and it was pretty clear they knew I was a faerie. A quiet voice from behind startled me.

"What is that, Lila?" Ash peered over my shoulder at the picture.

For the second time that day, I burst into tears and ran. I sprinted out of the building and across the parking lot. Footsteps pounded the pavement behind me. A hand gripped my arm and spun me around.

"Why were you sneaking up on me?" I shouted through my tears.

Ash removed his hand and stepped back to give me space. "I'm sorry. I wasn't trying to scare you. I wanted to talk to you, to apologize. For Lexie, for Finch's class, for everything. I've been kind of an ass today."

"Kind of? I don't think you could have been a bigger ass today if you'd tried." I took several deep breaths, trying to calm down.

Ash ran his hand through his dark hair, and I tried hard not to meet his eyes. Those eyes would suck me back in.

"I know," he said. "I was stupid. Wounded male pride, I guess."

He jammed his hands in his pockets and looked down as he kicked the ground. "It's just that I . . . I'm really into you, you know? I had even told my mom all about you, and she wants to meet you. So when you kicked me out last night, it kind of sucked."

"So you were a jerk because . . . you like me . . . and because I wasn't ready for you to touch me? Is that what you're saying?" I took a deep breath. This was so messed up.

"Yeah, when you say it like that, I really sound like an a-hole." He tried to catch my eyes. "It hurt to get turned down."

The anger subsided a little. "Ash, I wasn't turning you down. I'm sorry too, because I know I acted pretty strange." When he reached for my hand, I let him take it. "Trust me, I like you, too. It's kind of hard to explain—"

"Shhh . . . you don't need to say anything else."

I opened my mouth to speak but Ash dropped my hand. "Really, don't say anything else."

"But, why—"

"Is everything okay here? We saw you running." It was Mr. Turner, the assistant principal, followed closely by Ms. Gable.

"Yes, I'm fine." I answered, since they were focused on me rather than Ash. I must have looked like a wreck after my multiple sobbing spells. How many times would I have to lie that I was fine in one day? "I've had a rough day. Ash was trying to comfort me."

"Ah, yes," said Ms. Gable, "I guess it's good to have friends who care." She smiled, already looking back at Mr. Turner.

Mr. Turner studied us a moment. "Okay, then. Have a good weekend."

Ms. Gable stuck by his side as they walked away. I thought I heard her whisper "lovers' quarrel" before giggling like a schoolgirl.

I sighed. *Please don't let any other teachers ask me what's wrong today.* I was rooting for Ms. Gable, who seemed happier than ever, but I was glad she was gone.

I turned to Ash. "Thanks. I didn't know they were

behind me." A startling thought struck me. "But how did you know what I was going to say?"

"I didn't," said Ash, but he wouldn't meet my eyes. "I just figured it's nobody's business but ours."

I laced my fingers through his, feeling more bold now that he'd said out loud how he felt about me. "Drive me home after school?"

"Thought you'd never ask," Ash replied.

AFTER THE LAST BELL, Ash walked me to his truck, his hand in mine. It felt amazing. Basic human contact, whether hugs or hand holding, was something I'd feared and avoided for so long. I'd never even let my best friend hug me for fear she'd touch the bindings. I felt Ash's eyes on me, but for once I didn't care. I wanted to be seen. He opened the door for me and I hopped in, breathing in the artificial pine scent. I relaxed back against the seat.

Ash cleared his throat as he navigated his way through the parking lot. "So Lila," he said, "about that picture."

I stiffened beside him. "I'm not sure what to tell you. I don't know who put it there."

"Is it what I think it is?"

"I don't know," I lied. "I mean, they look like faerie wings, but I haven't heard of any more deaths. Have you?"

Ash shook his head. "No, and I watch the news every night." He paused. "Lila, why would someone put that in your locker?"

On one hand, I wanted nothing more than to tell him everything. However, I also saw how he'd reacted today when he was upset. What if another argument and his "wounded male pride" resulted in him telling the whole school about me? That would put my life in danger even more than it was.

I shrugged. "I guess someone thinks it's funny to put gross things in other people's lockers . . . trying to scare me, I guess."

Ash frowned and was silent the rest of the drive. I knew he didn't believe me, but he kept quiet. He pulled his buzzing cell phone out of his pocket, glanced at it, then put it back again. We parked at the curb by my house and walked up toward Mom's neat and orderly yard. Mrs. Nesbaum appeared like clockwork at the front gate. She must coordinate her gardening time with the end of the school day.

"Hello, Lila," she said in a loud voice.

"Hi, Mrs. Nesbaum. This is Ash," I said, trying to match her volume.

"Ash, is it?" she asked.

"Yes, ma'am. It's nice to meet you," said Ash.

Mrs. Nesbaum glanced down at our interlocked hands, winked at me and said, "My hearing may be going, but I'm not blind yet. That's quite a nice-looking young man you have there, Lila."

I flushed. If I could spend one day without blushing, crying, or running like I was on fire, it would be great. "Thanks. Well, we better get going."

"Bye, young ones. Take care." She turned her shears toward another rose bush.

"She seems nice," said Ash.

"Yeah, but she's *always* outside—I didn't think it was possible to tend roses as much as she does."

"Oh no, not a creepy rose tender. I hate neighbors like that." A teasing smile tugged at the corner of his mouth, and I gave him a playful punch.

I opened the mailbox and pulled out a stack of catalogs and bills. A red envelope caught my eye. It was addressed to me, but had no stamp or return address. I didn't know who'd delivered it but guessed it wasn't the neighborhood postman. The sick feeling returned as I stepped into the house and put the pile on the kitchen table. The red rectangle stared up at me. I wouldn't have thought it was possible for an envelope to look ominous, but this one did. Ash stood behind me, his hand on my shoulder.

"Hi, sweetie. Hello, Ash," Mom said, walking into the kitchen. "I just finished up for the day—" She stopped, following my gaze to the table. "What's wrong?"

I held up the thick envelope.

"What is it, Lila?" Her face looked pale.

"I don't know, but I guess I have to find out." Shaking, I tore the envelope. Inside was a card, *In Sympathy* written in flowery letters across the front. Before I could open it, picture after picture of bloody wings spilled out. Blue wings, pink wings, mint-green wings—all detached from their owners. I didn't need deductive reasoning to grasp that the killer didn't just know where I went to school, but also where I lived. I groaned, the card falling from my hand.

I heard a thud and turned to see Mom sprawled on the kitchen floor.

Ash ran to her and knelt by her side. He touched her head, calling out, "Ms. Kincade?"

I grabbed a dishtowel and soaked it in water. I bent over Mom, gently wiping her face with the cool towel until she opened her eyes.

Ash carried her to the couch despite her weak protests that she could walk. He propped up her feet with pillows, while I leaned her head back against the couch. Mom tried to sit up and put her hand to her head.

"Stop this, I'm fine," she said in an unconvincing voice. "What on earth is going on?"

I sighed and told her about the picture from the locker.

"Lila! How could you keep that from me?" She turned to Ash. "Maybe it's best if you leave, Ash."

I crossed my arms. "I don't want him to leave. Besides, you've kept tons of things from me 'for my own good.' I didn't want you to worry."

Mom rubbed her temple in small circles. "I'm your mom. It's my job to worry. Why is this happening to you?" Looking at Ash again, she opened her mouth but Ash spoke first.

He jammed his hands in his pockets. "I think it may have to do with me."

Mom and I both stared at him.

Mom's mouth dropped open. "What are you talking about?"

Ash swallowed. "Ms. Kincade, I think Lila may be in trouble because she's been hanging around with me. I'm not sure how to tell you this . . . I'm not sure I *should* tell you this."

"For the love of God, just say it," Mom begged.

Ash stepped closer to me, his eyes searching my face. "Lila, do you remember when I told you about my sister, Corrine?"

Remembering something about his having a sister in college, I nodded. He picked up my hand, ran his finger over the back of it, and turned to address Mom and me.

Ash took a deep breath. "My half-sister is a faerie."

16

ACTS OF REBELLION

I gasped and then hugged him tight. His sister was one of my kind—a faerie! That's why he had been so defensive about faeries the other day. I had to meet her. I had so many questions for her.

A horrible thought crossed my mind, and I pulled back. "Oh, Ash, all those pictures. Were any of the wings—"

"No. Corrine has dark rose-colored wings. I didn't see any like that." He reached into his pocket to grab his cell. "Also, she texts me every day since I . . . I worry about her. She's not like most faeries. I heard from her on the way over here. She's fine."

Mom studied him from the couch. "Ash, why would someone be sending the pictures to Lila, and not you, if they knew your sister was a faerie?"

Ash lowered himself into one of the armchairs and scratched his head. "I don't know. I haven't figured that out yet, but it's the only thing I can think of that would explain it."

"I have another explanation," I said. Staring at Ash, I

knew that no matter his reaction, I was ready to trust someone besides my mother. It was time to stop hiding.

"Lila Rose Kincade—don't you dare!"

"Mom, it's my choice. Someone obviously knows about me. To be honest, I don't understand why they haven't killed me already."

I walked over to the chair where Ash sat. My back faced Mom.

Keeping my eyes fixed on his, I said calmly, "Mom, unbind me."

"I will not! Have you lost your mind?" Mom fumbled to get off the couch.

Ash stood, gazing into my eyes. "I'll do it."

"You knew." My voice was quiet.

"Lila, I felt a connection with you from the second you gave me that mint in class, even before I knew what you were," he began.

My wings strained against my shirt. In a distant place, I heard my mother's defeated sigh.

He continued. "I didn't know about the faerie thing until today at your locker, when I saw that picture. Then things started clicking in my head—like your talk about half-faeries with Jacinda, and your soft hands. And how you wear loose shirts all the time, to hide the bindings, which is what Corrine used to do. It all added up."

"Why didn't you say anything?" I asked.

Ash touched my face. "Because of my sister. I grew up with all the secrecy stuff; I understand it. I figured you'd tell me when you felt safe enough—but when I saw those pictures, I thought if I told you about my sister, you'd know you could trust me."

I turned around and offered Ash my back. He lifted my shirt, taking care to only expose the bindings. He took off the tape in one smooth stroke and pulled down the fabric. It was the most exquisite unbinding I'd ever had.

My wings unfolded behind me and I pulled my shirt off.

"Lila Rose, have some decency," Mom protested.

I clutched my shirt in front of me, leaving my back bare. "This is who I am, Mom. Wings don't exactly lend themselves to shirts."

I heard the intake of breath from Ash. His fingers brushed my wings, and a tingling sensation ran through my entire body. The room around us glowed brighter as my wings sparkled under his touch.

"Whoa, I've never seen clear ones before."

"What do you mean?" I frowned at Ash.

Ash's eyes were fixed on my wings. "It's just that my sister's wings are pink, and her friends and the ones I've seen elsewhere are all different colors."

Mom excused herself, mumbling that she was finding me a suitable shirt to wear.

Ash ran his hand along one wing to the tip. "You are so beautiful."

I whirled around, holding my shirt to cover myself. "They are pretty, aren't they?"

"That's not what I said. They are amazing," said Ash, "but *you* are beautiful."

At that moment, Mom returned, thrusting an altered halter top into my hands. I raced to the bathroom to put it on, grateful that it allowed my wings some breathing room.

Mom's face was pinched with worry. "I'm terrified of what this all means. I'm leaning toward packing up and moving us to another state this instant."

"I won't go," I blurted. "I'm not going to run." My mind raced in an attempt to sort my options. We couldn't call the police; they hated faeries and relished enforcing the anti-mating laws. They'd be as likely to kill me as the killer. *Think, Lila, think.* The answer came like lightning. "Ash, you could take me to your sister. Maybe she could help." As I said it, I knew that meeting his sister was exactly what I needed to do—although I couldn't say why.

Ash considered this. "She is pretty well-connected, and it's less than a day's drive."

"Lila is not leaving my sight," Mom said. "Can't your sister come here?"

"Of course not," Lila interjected. "She'd be walking into murder central. You just said I'd be safer elsewhere, so I'd be safer than staying here. Besides, I'd be back in school on Monday. I'll be safer in a crowded school than at home. I—" Nausea slammed into me and I leaned over, gagging.

"What is it?" Mom and Ash asked in alarm.

I retched several more times before I cautiously stood up again. "Don't know. I just felt really sick for a minute. I think I'm okay now."

Mom studied me. "Are you sure? You've never been sick a day in your life."

"Yeah, I just need to rest a sec." I crashed down on the edge of the couch, and accidentally sat on the remote control. The television clicked on.

Mom reached for the controller.

"No, leave it on," I said. "It's the news."

The anchorwoman warned viewers about a drop in the temperature that would take place over the next few days. "The autumn air is about to get a lot colder. Join us after the break for Katie Sebring's full weather report."

After the commercial break, I couldn't help smiling at Katie's perky take on the weather, and my stomach slowly returned to normal. Ash sat beside me, rubbing my arm. Just as Katie started discussing the upcoming cold spell, a

Chapel Hill *Breaking News* banner flashed across the screen, cutting off her forecast mid-sentence.

"We interrupt this newscast to bring you breaking news. In a shocking turn of events related to the faerie murder several days ago, six more bodies have been found several miles north of the city, along Route 86. Several hikers stumbled across the grave in the Johnston Mill Nature Preserve early this morning. Judging by the marks on their back, they were all faeries, but their wings have not been found. We take you now to FBI Agent Heinrichsen, who is at the scene."

The FBI? I'd thought they only got involved in important cases. The screen changed to a tired-looking, husky man standing in front of a microphone. Behind him was a heavily treed area.

"Ladies and gentlemen, we are asking for your help. We hope that anyone with information about these crimes will come forward. Any tips you provide will remain confidential."

The camera then panned to another newscaster standing next to our governor. What the heck? The governor looked into the camera and leaned forward. "I would like to address the faeries out there."

I sat on the edge of the couch, anxious in my anticipation. Mom had voted for this guy because the prior governor was a total moron who tried to pass horrid laws against us. In my lifetime, no one had ever directly addressed faeries before. What could this guy have to say?

The governor stared into the camera. "I want to emphasize that it is our duty in the government to ensure the safety of *all* citizens. To all Americans—I implore you to embrace your winged neighbors. All should be considered equal regardless of race, religion, sexual preference, or species. We cannot tolerate hatred of any group, or we, who stand aside and do nothing, must share in the guilt with those committing the crimes."

I didn't realize tears were rolling down my cheeks until Mom wiped them away. Ash put his arm around me.

He continued. "As the safety of faeries cannot be guaranteed at this time, we have worked with the FBI to form the Faerie Protection Program. Agent Heinrichsen is spearheading the program. Notices are being sent to all registered faeries in the Triangle area. We strongly encourage you to seek refuge at an authorized FPP shelter until the matter is resolved. The shelter locations are confidential for obvious reasons, so please call the phone number on your screen for additional information, and have your registration number available."

The news alert ended, and Katie Sebring resumed her chipper weather report as if she hadn't heard a thing about mass murder. I turned off the TV and looked at Mom. "Registration number? I don't even know mine. Where is it?"

Mom stared at her lap. I pictured the government commercials I'd seen on television, where people were offered reward money for turning in unregistered faeries. *Unregistered=Unsafe* was the most popular slogan.

My eyes grew wide. "No way. I'm not registered? That's a serious crime—I could go to jail! I could—"

Mom raised her hand to stop me. "Lila, after the Faerie Wars, any doctor or midwife in the world delivering a baby with wings was mandated to report it to its government. When computer technology came about, all registration information was transferred to a centralized database in the US. Now faerie births are reported to the CDC—as if being a faerie was a sort of disease." She snorted. "I wasn't taking any chances with you. That's why I'm so strict about your bindings."

I couldn't hide my shock. Who knew Mom was so sly? "I guess I understand why I was a home birth."

"My mom felt the same way. Corrine's unregistered too," said Ash. "I'm hoping that means there are more faeries out there than people think."

I brought up visiting Ash's sister again, but Mom wouldn't hear of it. She said Ash could visit over the weekend, and that was good enough for me at the moment. Ash kissed me good-bye, but on the cheek, as Mom didn't leave the room. He whispered in my ear as he left, and it sounded an awful lot like he said, "See you later tonight."

Sophie's texts grew more insistent: *Hacksaw playing at 2p tomorrow. I'll swing by ur house to get u.*

Going to the movies was the last thing Mom would let me do: *I'm sick. Sorry.*

The phone rang immediately after I sent the text. I tried to sound as bad as I'd felt when I'd thrown up again. "Hey, Soph, I'm not blowing you off, I'm actually sick."

The annoyance in her voice was clear. "Ugh, you do sound sick. I really wanted to hang out tomorrow. . . . We haven't talked in forever. Maybe you'll be better in the morning?"

"Doubtful. My temp is 102 and I'm puking like crazy." I hated lying, especially to her.

"Gross. Well, I'm still checking in tomorrow; it could be a twenty-four-hour thing."

I hung up with Sophie in frustration. She should have been allowed to know the truth of what I am, and it shouldn't have mattered. It wasn't fair that I couldn't go the movies or wear a cute shirt like everyone else. Meeting Ash had unleashed something in me that made me not want to hide anymore. Which was problematic, what with a faerie killer being on the loose and all.

Mom stopped by my room on her way to bed, saying she needed to talk. She'd smudged the door on the way in and placed several new crystals of various colors on my windowsill "for protection." She perched next to me on my bed while I leaned back against my headboard.

"Don't take this the wrong way, Lila. It's just . . . well, don't you think it's a tad strange that all of this stuff started happening right when Ash started school? You've only known him a few days, after all. Are you sure he's one of the good guys?"

She tried to touch my face, and I leaned away from her. "Of course I am. Do you think I'm stupid—that I would blindly follow some random guy because he was cute?" Even as I spoke the words, I wondered. *Would I?*

"No, you're a very smart girl. All I'm saying is to be careful. The faeries who died might have trusted the killer too." Tears welled in Mom's eyes. "All this time trying to protect you, and I've failed." And it was true. She didn't go out much; she even hosted her friends at our house every month for book club.

My heart tugged at me, but I refused to cave. "Mom, you haven't failed—you're the reason I've been safe for so long. It's just that . . . people aren't meant to hide from the world." I straightened up and looked her directly in the eye. "Since we're being open and all, tell me the truth. How bad were the Faerie Wars?"

Mom rolled her eyes. "It's not like I was alive then."

"You know what I mean," I prodded. "Your generation heard more about it than mine."

She sighed and stared at the wall while she spoke. "I heard it was bad. They came here and after a short time, decided that humans were wrecking the planet and each other . . . which was honestly true, to an extent. They thought they deserved to take it over. I don't think they realized we would put up so much of a fight, being that we didn't have their magic. You're not at all like them, though, Lila, so don't feel badly. You're half-human—and your father was only a half-faerie at that."

I put my hand on her arm. "I know. I don't take it personally. It just helps me understand why people hate faeries so much." I frowned. "Although I have to say that humans have found plenty of wars to fight and plenty of people to be prejudiced against, way before we were around."

"That's very true." She studied me a moment longer, then smoothed my hair. "I should let you rest. You look exhausted." She handed me a small device and a container. "This is a very loud alarm, and this is mace. If anything seems out of the ordinary, hit the alarm; if someone comes in, spray them."

I nodded numbly. The thought of being attacked seemed surreal. I wasn't sure what good an alarm would do. Was Mom planning to come smudge the killer into submission?

As if reading my mind, she added, "Don't worry. I have more powerful things than mace in the house."

Mom had weapons other than large crystals? She'd managed to surprise me more today than in the last sixteen years of my life.

Mom had her hand on my door. "Lila? There's something else I need to tell you—"

The ringing of my phone interrupted her. His name

flashed across my cell. I showed it to her. "See, he's calling to check on me, so he must be good, right?"

Her expression was unreadable. "Go ahead and answer it. We'll talk more in the morning."

"M'kay. Love you, Mom." She'd barely closed the door when I hit Answer. "Ash?"

"Hey Lila, I've been thinking a lot. I have a proposition for you," he said. "I want you to come to Philadelphia with me for the weekend—to meet my sister."

My heart sank. "Yeah, I'd love to . . . but you heard my mom. No way will she let me go."

There was momentary silence on the other end. "Lila, not that I want to disrespect your Mom, but I think this trip is important. Maybe she'd understand better after you got back and explained it to her."

What? He was asking *me* to sneak out of my house and leave town for the weekend. Me, the girl who didn't dare enter class without her homework, the girl who went to bed at nine thirty so she'd be adequately rested for class, the girl whose last rebellious act occurred at the age of *five*. Meeting another faerie would be beyond my wildest dreams, but I wasn't that girl.

"I can't. I'm sorry. Please don't be mad." I really wished I were that girl.

"Lila, I'm not mad. I'm worried about you. I'll come over tomorrow."

After hanging up, I hopped online to make sure faerie parts weren't being auctioned off again. Nothing on eBay but several faerie trinkets and a bumper sticker by a religious group that read *Tinker Bell is from Hell*. Yawning, I exited eBay and reached for the power button, when a banner flashed across the screen. *Breaking News: Another brutal faerie murder today in the Research Triangle.* My stomach dropped.

I dialed Ash's number and he answered after the first ring. "Lila, are you okay?"

My heart raced as I responded. "I changed my mind. When can we leave?"

DREAMIN' AND SCREAMIN'

T he warm ocean breezes caress my face and I smile. They fall so easily; it's like snapping sticks. Their screams echo through the air as frail, dead bodies litter the ocean below me. I am invincible. There is only one left. Only one more and it will be done, yet it is far away, and I cannot see its face. The sun casts a bright glare around its body. I can't even tell if the freak is male or female. Though it doesn't move away from me, I cannot seem to get closer. Unlike the others, this one doesn't scream. I'll fix that. I lunge at it, attempting to tear off its wings, but no matter how hard I try . . . I can't quite kill it.

BLINKING, I sit up in bed. I punch my pillow, growling in anger. It's just a dream, I tell myself.

I grab the keys from my bedside table. It's time to go for a drive.

PINK AND PROUD

We drove under a moonless sky, speeding through the night as though a demon was chasing us. Though I'd hastily written Mom a note while Ash bound my wings, telling her not to worry and that I'd call, the guilt and anxiety sat like a stone in my gut.

"It'll be okay," Ash promised, squeezing my hand.

Though I doubted anything would be okay, I reminded myself why I was doing this. The fact that I got to spend a whole weekend with Ash *and* meet another faerie was the silver lining to a very dark cloud. Plus, there was something exciting about venturing outside North Carolina for the first time in my life. I was going to a city I'd only ever seen in a snow globe.

I squeezed back. "Ash? What did you mean at my house when you said your sister's not like other faeries?"

Ash laughed. "My sister is a vocal advocate, emphasis on the vocal part, for the rights of faeries—and any other disenfranchised group. She's not afraid of a good fight. In fact, I've never seen her back down in my life."

I was awestruck. "She admits she's a faerie to other people? I wish I could be that brave. I've stayed quiet so I wouldn't rock the boat."

"Yeah, my sister is the boat-rocking queen. She also makes the best sweet tea you've ever had. You can take the girl out of North Carolina, but you can't take North Carolina out of the girl." Ash smiled again. "I think you'll like her—a lot."

"Of course I'll like her—she's related to you."

Ash grinned. "I hope so. I've never introduced a girlfriend to my sister before."

My head swiveled toward him. "Wait a sec, did you just call me your girlfriend?"

Ash's cheeks turned pink. Was he actually blushing? He glanced over at me. "Yeah, I guess I did. What do you think about that?"

My first ever boyfriend? What did I think about that? It was impossible to keep from smiling ear to ear. "It's cool. I'm good with that. Now tell me more about your sister."

Ash laughed, then started talking. I couldn't get enough of the details, so I just let Ash talk as I soaked it all in. After a few hours, we pulled over and changed seats so I could drive, but I couldn't help checking and rechecking the rearview window to make sure we weren't being followed. "So, what happened with Corrine's dad?"

Ash gazed out the window at the reflectors dotting the road. "My mom was married to him and . . . they really loved each other. Of course it was a secret wedding and not really legal, given the mating laws and all, but they made it work."

Ash looked over at me and bit his lip as if deciding whether or not to continue. Turning back to the road in front of him, he said, "One day when Corrine was still a baby, he disappeared—never came home. My mom was devastated. The authorities thought he abandoned them, but my mom knew he wouldn't do that."

Sounds familiar. "How awful."

Ash rested his hand on my leg. "Yeah, speaking of that, I better call my mom and let her know what's going on." The sound of his voice made my eyes grow heavier, and I yawned, fighting to keep focused on the road ahead.

After another hour, we switched spots again so Ash could drive. My head fell back against the headrest, and the motion of the tires on the bumpy highway soon lulled me to sleep.

THE WOODS WERE MURKY. A pale moon cast an eerie glow over us. Ash whispered in my ear, urging me to keep going. I wanted to turn back, but his hand was on my back, pushing me forward. There was an old wooden shack ahead in the distance, its front door mostly obscured by shadows. I didn't want to go in—something terrible was on the other side. We stood at the entrance as the wind whipped around us. A cold rain fell, and I couldn't stop shivering. The door opened by itself on creaky hinges that screeched through the forest. I attempted to run but was frozen in place. I tried to scream but nothing came out. Something pulled me through the doorway from the other side. I fell into blackness.
. .

"LILA, WAKE UP! YOU'RE DREAMING." Ash had one hand on the wheel while he gently shook me with his other.

I struggled to pull myself from sleep. Ash's voice helped me to escape the sinister shack. I opened my eyes, turning to him. "Bad dream," I managed.

"Yeah, it didn't seem like a good one." He massaged my arm as though he could somehow erase the visions in my head. "It's going to be okay."

"I hope you're right." A chill went through me. "I don't have a great feeling, though."

We pulled off the highway at the next exit for gas and the restroom, the neon lights of the service station buzzing in the dark. I stretched my legs, trying to ignore the soreness in my back. Nighttime was usually when my wings were free —it was super painful for them to be restrained this long. But I couldn't risk leaving them unbound in the car, even at nighttime. If the headlights of another car hit Ash's truck at the right angle, my wings would light up like a Christmas tree angel.

I popped a few ibuprofens in the convenience store and washed them down with some bottled water, hoping it would take the edge off. Ash flipped shut the door to the gas tank as I came up behind him, leaning my head against his shoulder.

"I'll drive now," I said. "After that dream, I don't even want to go back to sleep. Besides, you look exhausted."

Ash nodded. "Yeah, I'm pretty beat. Maybe I will catch a few z's. Wake me in an hour, though." He kissed me before dropping into his seat. "Seriously, wake me if you need me."

I flipped on the radio to distract myself with music, keeping the volume low enough so Ash could sleep. He snored softly beside me, and I pretended we were going off on vacation together. Somewhere with cotton candy and roller coasters, not serial killers and dead faeries.

～

DAYLIGHT CREPT over the horizon as the sky took on a pinkish tinge. Ash stretched in the seat next to me. "Hey, you were supposed to wake me in an hour."

My wings woke at the sound of his voice. I smiled, grateful I'd taken the painkillers earlier. "You looked so peaceful. You hungry?"

"Starving."

We located a fast-food place off the highway, and Ash offered to drive since we were getting close to his sister's place. A few minutes later, we were back on the road with egg sandwiches and coffee. A "Pennsylvania Welcomes You" sign came into view.

"Not long now," Ash said.

His cell phone buzzed. I grabbed it for him and squealed at the text. "It's from Corrine. She says everything is great and to text when we're close. I'm on it."

I'd barely handed his phone back when mine rang. Since Ash was with me, it had to be either Sophie or Mom. I groaned when I checked the caller ID.

"Answer it," said Ash. "Blame it on me. Say I kidnapped you or something."

I groaned and answered. "Mom, before you say anything . . . no, listen . . . stop, I'm fine, I swear . . . yes, I heard about it. That's why I decided to leave with Ash. I'm safer away from there, plus, I really need to meet his sister. No, stay there . . . seriously, someone could follow you here . . . I'll keep in touch, and I'll be back home by Monday, I promise . . . I have to go, Mom. Love you."

"Well, that went super well," I said, and sighed.

"She'll be fine," said Ash. "Until Monday. But you may decide it's safer to stay out of town. It's your call."

Shock ran through me. I hadn't considered leaving long-term. Mom and everything else in my life was back home. But the killings were happening in North Carolina, so maybe staying away was the smarter move. I'd figure something out by Monday.

I stared out the window, trying to clear my head, and surveyed my surroundings. The trees hadn't yet started to change colors, but the green leaves would soon give way to intricate oranges, reds, and golds. The cool air swept through my hair. I tingled with excitement about meeting Corrine. As usual, just when the slightest feeling of happiness crept in, a terrible thought followed.

"Ash? Corrine sounds so different from me. What if she doesn't like me?"

He laughed. "I know my sister. She'll love you, trust me."

We turned up the radio and sang along in loud voices. I reveled in this experience of new places, new feelings, and didn't want it to end. Of course, it would be helpful if someone didn't want me dead, but they hadn't actually tried to kill me yet. They seemed to be teasing me—or testing me. Why was that?

"You're not singing anymore, which tells me you're worrying instead," said Ash. He'd dialed the volume down. "What's up?"

"You know me pretty well for someone I just met this week."

Ash smiled. "I feel like I've known you a lot longer than that. Don't worry, this will turn out fine."

My wings pulsed underneath my shirt. "I hope so."

We turned down a narrow one-lane wooded road. After driving several miles through the trees, Ash rounded a bend in the road and slowed down. "Here we are."

He pulled into the driveway of a large stone house with

ivy climbing its walls. A face peered through the window, and we heard a shriek of delight from inside the house. We'd scarcely reached the front door when it swung in, opened by a shy-looking girl. Behind the girl, I heard Corrine before I saw her. A whooshing sound of wings echoed through the room. A blur of rose on a pink-haired faerie hovered above us.

No way . . . she's flying!

"Little bro, I'm so glad you're here! It's been ages." Corrine landed and enveloped her younger brother in a bear hug.

Ash grinned. When they let go, he gestured to me. "Corrine, this is Lila."

It was my turn to be enfolded in her powerful embrace. Corrine beamed at me. "You have no idea how happy I am to meet you."

I stared at Corrine, open-mouthed. "But . . . you just . . . you . . . flew."

"Of course I flew. That is what the wings are for, honey." Corrine winked at me, motioning for them to come into the main room. "C'mon, I want you to meet the others."

I stared with envy at Corrine's cute fitted top with two slits cut in the back for her wings. It had to be from Winged. Corrine didn't seem to care about blending into the woodwork—her hair was platinum blond with hot pink highlights. Ash wasn't kidding when he said his sister wasn't a wallflower.

We walked into a main room decorated with cozy leather furniture and antique rugs. I gasped and dropped my bag. Faeries and humans lounged side by side on the furniture. The faeries' wings were displayed with no sign of shame on their faces. In fact, not a trace of discomfort could be detected on anyone's face, except mine.

"You okay? You look like you've seen a ghost." Corrine looked concerned.

I gulped. "Well, it's just that . . . you can't . . . you're living openly with humans. I mean, the government could kill you for being out of Hiding."

One wingless girl responded, "Hiding, schmiding. We're all roommates here. So, I'm human and Corrine is faerie—big deal. We're much more alike than we are different."

"Yeah," said a boy, "Like we all have to study our asses off to pass our history final next week." Everyone laughed.

"So, do you go to class like that?" Why hadn't I seen these renegade faeries plastered across the Internet?

"Not yet. The world's not quite ready for that, but we're getting there," said Corrine. "But here around the house, and a few other places, we're free to be ourselves. It's our small oasis amid a sea of insanity," she said, gesturing toward the world outside. "This is our sanctuary."

"I'm in awe. I wish I had your freedom," I said.

A faerie who introduced herself as Brooklyn was perched on the end of the couch. Petite, with icy blue wings and raven hair, she looked like a textbook faerie—like she'd stepped out of a kids' movie. "Not everyone is as prejudiced as the raving lunatics you hear about on TV, calling us 'unnatural mutations.'" She smiled at me. "Look at Ash—he seems to like you the way you are."

Ash grinned. "I most definitely like you exactly how you are."

Corrine made introductions around the room. There were two other faeries in addition to Corrine and Brooklyn. One was a solemn-looking female named Jessa, and one of them, Gabriel, was male. I had to admit, I'd never thought of male faeries as, well, manly. It was time to rethink that. Now I understood my mother's indiscretion so many years ago. Gabriel was muscular, with dark-as-night skin, piercing eyes, and hair in tight braids that hung to his shoulders. He sat next to Sarah, the shy human girl who'd opened the door, his finger twined through her blond hair. They looked so cozy—they were totally violating the anti-mating laws.

A taller guy walked over to us. "Hi, I'm Paul," he said, thrusting his hand out toward me. He winked. "Corrine's human boyfriend."

"Oh, sorry, yes, I forgot," Corrine said. "He knows Ash already."

I shook his hand, making a note of how many human-faerie couples were making it work.

"I'll show you two to your room so you can get settled," said Corrine.

I looked at Ash and back at Corrine. "Room—not rooms?" I asked.

Corrine chortled. "You are too cute. Don't worry, there are two beds."

"Although I wouldn't kick you out of mine if you wanted to share," teased Ash.

"Ha, ha." I gave him a playful shove.

Corrine led us down a hallway and up the stairs. We passed by a room with a vaulted ceiling, a big leather couch, and floor-to-ceiling bookshelves.

I was awestruck. "Wow, that's amazing. You have your own library?"

"Sure do. It's not like any library you've ever seen either —I guarantee that," said Corrine. "I'll show you later. We all pooled together for this house, along with a generous dona-tion from Gabriel's family. The plan is to make it a long-term safe house of sorts."

She led us to a room at the far end of the hallway. Spare

but spacious, it did, in fact, contain two double beds. I placed my bag on an antique quilt covering one of the beds.

"The bathroom is down the hall; you share it with the room next door. That's Gabriel and Sarah's room." Corrine smiled at us. "See, they've been together three years now, so relationships between humans and faeries can work out just fine."

"What about the anti-mating laws?" I asked. "Aren't you afraid you'll get caught?"

Corrine snorted. "I don't follow arcane laws created by Nazis. Besides, the only real proof of mating is a baby. Use protection, and there's nothing for them to know." She winked. "I'll leave you two to rest a bit after your all-nighter on the road—we'll have an early dinner about three or so." Corrine stopped to survey Lila from head to toe. "Oh, but you can't come like that, you look so uncomfortable. Aren't your wings aching to be out?"

I nodded. "You have no idea."

"Okay, I'll be right back." Corrine flew out the door.

My eyes followed her. "I can't get over the fact that she's flying. I've had it drilled into my head my whole life that flying is forbidden."

"Corrine is right," said Ash. "That's sort of the purpose of wings—they weren't meant to be bound."

Corrine flew back in, breathless, and landed at my feet holding a top that would make Miranda jealous. No one wearing this would be on anyone's worst-dressed list. Corrine flipped it around to show the holes in back.

"Here, honey. This will feel so much better." She handed it to me. "It'll *look* a heck of a lot better too," she said laughing.

Ash hugged his sister again. "I'm so glad we're here, and that you're safe."

"It'll take more than a maniacal madman to take me down," Corrine said with a shrug. Then she flew off, back to the others.

"She's amazing," I said.

"Yeah, that's my big sis."

My phone buzzed. Sophie. I texted her that I was so sick I couldn't talk, and would call her later. Then I texted Mom telling her that I was fine and would call later, and set the phone on the dresser. The phone buzzed immediately, but I didn't want to talk.

"Is it bad that I already feel like I don't want to leave here?" I asked, turning back to Ash.

"No. Corrine has a way of making you feel like you're home," said Ash. "Now how 'bout I unbind those wings so you can change into something more fashionable?"

I offered my back to Ash. He kissed my shoulder as he removed the fabric from my grateful wings. He averted his eyes while I pulled my shirt over my head and replaced it with the cute lavender top. "So, what do you think?"

His eyes scanned my body, and a low whistle escaped his lips. Our eyes met, and the intensity of his stare made me shiver. I stepped back from him and turned to the bed, mumbling something about needing to sleep.

His arm circled around me from behind, and he kissed the back of my neck. "Seriously, you look amazing."

My freed wings responded with rapid beating and one wing smacked Ash right in the face. He laughed. "Ow! Guess that'll teach me not to get too close." But he didn't let go.

I turned and kissed him lightly. "We barely slept all night. We really should rest a little."

He nipped at my bottom lip. "Sleep with me. I'll behave. I just want to feel you next to me."

Twist my arm. I curled up next to him and drifted into a sound sleep, waking only when he nudged me to say it was time for lunch. My wings were folded underneath me, and he was careful not to lean on them when he sat up.

I laughed. "It's okay. They're stronger than they look. Trust me, you won't hurt them."

He stroked one wing. "They feel so delicate—different from Corrine's."

"Maybe, but they're so strong they've never had so much as a tiny tear in them, even after all these years of having tape ripped off them every day." I walked to the mirror and ran my hand through my hair.

"Shall we?" he asked, holding out his arm.

"We shall." With my arm linked through his, we descended the stairs together. I didn't feel quite ready to fly in front of others, and was content just having my wings out in the open. We followed the scent of baked chicken to the dining room. A huge pitcher of what I hoped was sweet tea adorned the table. My mouth watered.

"Ta-da. What do you think?" I asked, twirling around. My wings lit up the room, glowing brighter than ever.

Brooklyn dropped the silverware she'd been holding. It clattered to the hardwood floor, echoing across the room. Gabriel's muscular body flinched. Jessa glared at me like I had come straight from hell. Paul looked from them to me, confusion etched across his face.

Corrine stared at me, her face pale against her pink hair. Was that a warning glance she flashed the others? "Love the shirt, Lila. Let's eat."

The food was amazing, and I learned a lot as the conversation varied between discussion of the murders and faerie lore, yet something seemed off. Had seemed off from the moment I'd walked in wearing Corrine's top. *What the hell?*

Maybe they thought I was just a dumb high school kid who didn't measure up to their fancy college standards, but they hadn't acted that way earlier. I'd hoped that if I met other faeries, I'd finally fit in somewhere. Maybe that was wishful thinking. Maybe I'd never fit in.

19

THE UNDERGROUND

Paul brought in bowls of chocolate mousse with raspberries and whipped cream for dessert. It was perfect—airy and light—but I could barely make myself swallow.

Ash gulped his down in several bites. "Geez, Paul, this is awesome."

Paul smiled. "Thanks, it's one of my specialties."

Brooklyn licked her spoon. "Why are all your specialties desserts? They are so good but so bad for my faerie figure."

"More faerie figure to love," Corrine said, "besides, it's not every day my baby brother visits and brings us a new faerie friend."

Jessa coughed in a sudden spasm, like her mousse had gone down the wrong way.

An awkward silence descended on the table. Ash seemed oblivious as he licked his spoon. I pushed my chair back, eager to escape to my room, when Corrine dropped her spoon with a clatter.

All heads turned toward her.

"I have a great idea," she announced.

Gabriel leaned back in his chair. "All your ideas are great. Let's hear it."

Was that a flicker of annoyance on Sarah's face?

"We're going to show Lila here a good time. A really good time. Got it?"

"Yes!" Gabriel pumped his fist in the air.

Paul cleared his throat. "Corrine, are you sure? Is that really a safe place to bring guests?"

Corrine raised an eyebrow. "Damn straight. She needs to see we are making progress in more places than our own home. Plus, it's a hoot."

Gabriel jumped up. "Hell yeah, let's do this."

"Do I have to go?" Jessa asked.

"C'mon, Jessa," said Sarah. "Even you have fun there. It'll be great."

Jessa crossed her arms but didn't protest.

I looked at Ash, who seemed as confused as I was. If they truly didn't like me, they wouldn't invite me out with them, right? I turned back to Corrine. "Where are we going?"

Corrine's eyes twinkled across the table. "The Underground."

LATER THAT NIGHT, we packed into Jessa's giant SUV and made our way through the streets of Philly until we reached an area that looked like an abandoned warehouse district. I'd called Mom right before we left and given her a brief rundown about Ash's sister and reassured her that I was fine —I left out the bit about going to party at a faerie club. She was tearful but sounded resigned. I promised I would call again when I had more time to tell her everything. Or almost everything.

Jessa stared straight ahead at the road and didn't speak to anyone during the drive there. The vehicle was beyond cramped due to all the free-flying wings inside. All except mine.

My bindings, done by Ash, were firmly in place as always—my cute Winged top replaced by the bulky sweatshirt I'd worn on the drive from Chapel Hill. "Remind me again why everyone else is allowed to be free tonight?"

Another moment of uncomfortable silence. Ash had told me before we left the house that everything was fine, and that I was just being too sensitive.

"They know us at this place, honey," said Corrine. "They don't know you. It's safer for you to look human for now."

Brooklyn flashed me a reassuring smile.

We pulled into the parking lot of what, by all accounts, looked to be a deserted building. Even the parking lot was empty. My heart started beating faster.

"Relax, cupcake." Gabriel patted my arm. "It's all good."

Jessa pulled up to the dark entrance of the building, while Corrine whipped out her phone and sent a text to someone.

A minute later, a hulking man marched out the front door and everyone clamored out of the SUV. Ash gripped my hand. "No idea what this place is, but if Corrine says it's great, then it has to be."

Sarah smiled at me, her hand entwined with Gabriel's. "Don't worry. They park the vehicles in back, so you can't see them from the road."

Jessa handed her keys to the man, who eyed me and Ash.

Corrine smiled at the guy. "It's just my bro and his girl-friend. They're fine."

Being called Ash's girlfriend was never going to get old. After a pause, he nodded and gestured us all inside.

When we approached the front door, I saw that it—and all the windows—were painted black. We stepped through the entrance and were met with an eerie silence, though the hallway vibrated with a pulsing sensation. I didn't understand it until Gabriel threw open the second door at the end of the hall and ushered us onward.

Music blared in the huge room as throngs of humans and faeries alike danced to a techno beat, orchestrated by a faerie DJ with electric-blue hair who hovered over her equipment at the back. Large mirrors covered several walls, and a bar was off to the right, where everyone jostled for drinks. There were so many different-colored wings, and the light reflecting off all of them in the mirrors created a colored strobe light effect in the room.

My mind reeled. Faeries and humans were partying in public together. It was unthinkable. Seeing all the faeries being out made me want to be too. My wings began pulsing with the beat of the music in their bindings. Corrine's excuse for why I had to stay bound didn't fly with me. Something still felt wrong.

Gabriel grabbed Sarah's hand. "Let's get our dance on," he said over the music.

Corrine nodded. "I'm getting a drink first."

"Me too," said Jessa quickly.

"Y'all want a Coke?" Corrine asked me and Ash. "Paul, a beer?"

I shook my head. All I could do at the moment was gawk. Corrine flew to the bar, but Jessa walked, her wings flapping unused behind her.

Paul smiled at Ash and me while we waited for them.

"You both look a little overwhelmed. I take it you've never been to a place like this before?"

Ash had my hand firmly in his. "That's an understatement. How does this place stay open? Why don't the cops shut it down?"

"They would certainly try," Paul said. He gestured around the room. "The Underground rotates to different locations, and they don't let anyone in they don't know. Someone has to vouch for you if the bouncer doesn't recognize you."

Brooklyn nodded. "The system works, and it gives us a chance to have some fun."

It was hard to hear them over the music, so we stepped closer. Paul looked over to where Corrine and Jessa waited at the bar. Two faerie bartenders, one male and one female, flew back and forth pouring drinks and taking orders.

"I do worry, though," Paul admitted. "She's such a fighter, which I love, but I'm afraid she'll get in over her head one of these days. And with a killer out there now . . ."

"At least we're safe here," Ash said. "We're hundreds of miles away from all that."

Though we technically were in fact, hours away from North Carolina, I didn't feel as safe as I thought I would. Maybe it was those dreams, where the killer found me no matter where I was.

Corrine flew back carrying a pink drink with an umbrella sticking out of it. She landed lightly and took a sip. "Delicious!" she declared.

Jessa walked over with a shot glass in each hand.

"What is that?" Paul asked.

"Bourbon." She threw back the first shot, followed closely by the second.

"Take it easy," Corrine said.

Paul shook his head. "Guess I'm the designated driver tonight."

Jessa put the shot glasses on a nearby table and wiped her mouth with her arm. "Perfect, because I don't intend to be sober for long."

Ash shot me a look. "C'mon, Lila, let's dance."

"Yes, go on, you two," Corrine urged, as Paul put a protective arm around her. "Lila, you need to have some fun." She leaned closer to me. "And I promise you, I will bring you back here again when your wings can be free. Deal?"

I wanted to ask her why they couldn't be now, but I just nodded. "Deal."

Ash and I went out on the dance floor. The energy in the room buzzed, and I drank it all in. Some faeries danced on the floor with their human counterparts, and some hovered in the air and zipped down to the floor and back up again.

Ash tilted my face toward his and I started to move, hesitantly at first. Though I had flown once in my life in childhood, I had never danced. I'd never felt free enough to let go like this. He put his hand on my hip and pulled me closer to him. We moved in rhythm, and as the music washed over me, I danced faster. I stared into Ash's eyes and smiled, no longer caring about the fact that I wore a sweatshirt while everyone else was dressed for clubbing.

Song after song came on, and Ash and I danced. Sweat ran down the inside of my sweatshirt, but I didn't care. The only thing that would have made this night better was setting my wings free, but I vowed to come back again and do just that. In fact, if I'd had a shirt available, I'd go let my wings out now, no matter what anyone else thought.

Gabriel still danced nearby, but I didn't see Sarah with

him. The song ended and I wiped sweat from my forehead as Gabriel joined us.

"I'm getting a glass of water," I said. "Be right back."

"I'll go with you," Ash said.

"No, I got it. Stay with Gabriel—I'm fine." I walked toward the bar, feeling weirdly rebellious. I was in a dance club walking to get water on my own. Sophie walked to and from school with me, Mom was always with me at the house, and I was constantly surrounded by classmates at school. If this was what independence felt like, I liked it. A lot.

A female faerie with sunshine-yellow wings flew above me toward the bar area, then turned back to me and landed at my side. She lightly touched my bulky sweatshirt. "I've been there too. Not long ago, in fact. Don't worry, you'll find a lot of support here when you choose to come out." She smiled and flew away again.

But I want to come out, I wanted to yell. As I pushed closer to the bar, I noticed Sarah off to the side by the corner, texting.

"Hey, Sarah!" I waved to her as I got closer to her and reached the bar.

She shoved the phone into her pocket. "Hi, Lila."

The male bartender flew to me and I got a big glass of water. I stepped over to Sarah. "Are you having fun?" I asked.

"Yeah, I guess," she said. "I'm not a big partier, but Gabriel loves this place." She gazed across the room. "But I never get tired of seeing all these beautiful wings." She sighed. "Faeries are the best."

I laughed. "That's something I don't hear very often."

Sarah snapped her gaze back to me and looked uncomfortable. Or was it guilty?

"Have you seen Jessa?" I asked.

Sarah pointed to the other end of the bar. Jessa leaned against a chair, with numerous empty shot glasses in front of her. She was talking to the bartender, but he shook his head at her.

"Looks like someone got cut off," Sarah said.

Jessa stormed away from the bar, stumbling as she went.

I turned back to Sarah. She had her phone in her hand again but put it back in her pocket after she glanced at the screen.

"You and Gabriel seem really happy," I said.

She frowned. "Yeah, I really like him a lot, and he's super hot . . . but sometimes, it's hard to date a faerie . . . even though I love them and all."

Interesting that she said *them*, not him. I stared at her.

"I mean, it's complicated. I have really racist family members who would disown me if they knew about Gabriel. And the whole serial killer thing is way creepy."

My great mood evaporated as reality set back in, along with the sudden thought that Gabriel deserved better. I shifted from one foot to the other. "Yeah, uh, I have to go to the bathroom. I'll be back."

She nodded and pulled out her phone as I left.

I texted Ash while I waited in line for the restroom. He said he and Gabriel were with Corrine, Brooklyn, and Paul. I told him where Sarah was but had no idea what had happened to Jessa.

When I finally made it into a stall, I heard someone puking in the one next to me, then moaning.

"Jessa?"

She mumbled in response, then vomited again. So faeries could get sick. I guess I'd just been really lucky up until the last few months. Weird.

I waited outside her stall until she was done, and she finally came out, her wings limp.

"Are you okay?" I asked.

"Obviously not." She made it to the sink. Drunk Jessa was no nicer than sober Jessa.

I handed her a paper towel so she could wipe a chunk from her cheek.

Ash texted, and I told him I had Jessa and would be out in a minute.

"I think we're ready to go. I can help you out if you want."

Jessa tossed the paper towel in the trash with a harsh laugh. "Like you could help me. The great savior faerie, Lila."

"What does that mean?" I couldn't even save myself, let alone anyone else. She ignored me, and anger rose up inside me. "What is your problem? You're a faerie too, but you act like we're all scum." I marched toward the door.

"You know who wasn't scum? My big sister." Jessa teetered after me, steadying herself once against the wall. "Went on the vacation-of-a-lifetime to London and didn't come back. She was killed. All because of having wings. Wings bring nothing but trouble."

She tripped over her own foot and went down on the dirty tiles. "Fuckin' faeries," she muttered, and threw up on the floor . . . and her feet.

20

BOOK OF FAERIE

A sh slept soundly that night, his arm around my waist, his warm breath against my ear. I couldn't sleep, the events of the night replaying over and over in my head. The clock on the bedside table read 1:00 a.m. I shifted toward the edge of the bed. Ash yawned and rolled over, away from me. I sat up, placing my feet on the hardwood floor next to the bed. No sounds could be heard from anywhere in the house.

For reasons I couldn't explain, I was drawn to the library. I would have asked to go there earlier, but it wasn't like people were throwing down the welcome mat at my feet. Ash had told me that I was being overly sensitive and that everything was fine. Yes, I might be sensitive, but everything was not fine, and I intended to find out why.

The hallway was immersed in darkness, only a faint glimmer shining up from some small electronic gadget downstairs. I stopped to listen outside Gabriel and Sarah's door, then moved down the corridor, feeling my way along the wall. A floorboard creaked underfoot and I froze, waiting a minute until I felt it was safe before continuing onward. The library was the next door down. As I reached the door, a slight breeze lifted my wings. God, it felt good. *No one would see me if I flew, just this once.* Stifling the urge, I pushed open the library door, then closed it gently behind me.

I groped around with my hands until I located the couch. Near it was a small end table with a lamp. I switched it on, and a soft, warm light filled the center of the room. Hundreds of books adorned shelves that lined the walls, reaching up to the rafters. Several moving ladders attached to metal rails at the top of the shelves. The large leather couch was flanked by several matching armchairs. A frosted glass coffee table sat in the middle, and matching antique lamps adorned two end tables on either side of the couch. Gabriel's parents must have donated quite a stash to pay for all this. It was the most inviting room I'd ever seen. Too bad it felt more like I was trespassing than visiting.

I started browsing the bookshelves closest to the door. I slowly circled the room, gazing at each row of books, pulling some out and leafing through them before setting each one back in its spot. They all appeared to either be about faeries or written by faeries, and were grouped in sections. There was a faerie fiction section, and I smiled when I spotted Shakespeare in there. Another bookcase held faerie nonfiction and memoir. Ella Tatiana's book held a prominent position smack in the center of the row, sitting with its cover facing the room. I wondered how many of these books had been banned.

Though I knew something I needed was in this room, I also knew I hadn't found it yet. I continued walking around the perimeter of the room. The bookcase farthest from the door was different from the others. It had a front panel that rose two feet from the floor, so its shelves started farther up than the rest of them. I bent down and touched the wooden panel. It was smooth and polished under my fingers. I knocked lightly; the interior of the bookshelf sounded hollow.

I slid my fingers along the sides of the bookcase until I hit a small notch in the wood. I pushed on the notch and heard a clicking sound. The front panel of the bookcase popped open. I opened the panel wider and peered inside. The interior of the bookcase was inhabited by a small, glass-enclosed cabinet. The cabinet contained two rows of ancient-looking books. I pulled the small glass doors toward me and removed several of the books. History books about the faerie realm.

My wings buzzed. I was close. After I'd removed all the books from the cabinet, I thumbed through a few, but I knew I'd need weeks to read all these books. I didn't have weeks; I didn't even have days. Maybe I'd sneak one into our room and read what I could before we had to leave. As I put some of the books back into the shelf, I noticed a small indentation in the back of the glass case. It couldn't be. Why would somebody need a secret compartment within a secret compartment? I put my finger in the indentation and pushed. Nothing happened. Then I moved my finger sideways, and the back door slid open.

Inside was a lone book, a thick tome with a faded maroon cover embossed with gilded lettering. Despite its obvious age, it was the most beautiful book I had ever seen. I ran my hand over the leather cover and stared at the ornate letters. *Book of Faerie.* No author was listed anywhere in it. This, I knew, was what I'd been looking for.

I curled up on the couch and began reading. *Holy cow.* This wasn't just any history book. It was written by the Pure Ones, before they ever came to Earth. It contained a wealth of information about the history of faeries. Though this book appeared to be hundreds of years old, one of the first things I learned was that there was no time in the faerie realm. Time didn't exist there.

I read tales of primeval wars in the faerie realm, accompanied by vivid drawings, interspersed with biographies of important Pure Ones. Parts of it were disturbing. There were several accounts of travels to other worlds—worlds they had conquered for the sheer fun of it. It seemed a sort of challenge for them to see how quickly they could use their magic to overtake a land or planet. They often chose places that had the properties of space and time; it gave them the chance to experience something different from their own realm. Besides the faerie realm, Pure Ones owned the equivalent of an entire solar system, where they moved freely between worlds. As I read through their various conquests, I realized that none of the wars with other species involved their own defeat. No wonder they thought Earth would be a piece of cake to take over—they'd never lost.

Then I came across the story of a Pure One named Saharie. Saharie wanted to take the throne away from Galem, the reigning Pure One. Badly. Declaring war on him, she thrust her knife into him—and killed them both instantly. Saharie had unknowingly died by suicide; she hadn't known that Pure Ones share a symbiotic energy source. That a Pure One who attempts to harm another will harm themselves as well—the disruption of energy surges back at the faerie who violates the flow.

Hearing a noise outside the quiet room, I sat up straighter. I tilted my head to the side, listening. A minute passed, but after hearing nothing more, I chalked it up to my fatigued mind playing tricks on me.

I devoured as much of the book as I could. Each Pure

One had a different magical ability, sort of like how no two snowflakes are exactly alike, which was part of why they were harder to kill. I read deep into the night until the words began to blur on the page. Yawning, I flipped to the next section—the significance of dreams for faeries. There were several hundred pages left, and my eyes refused to read any more. I'd have to find a way to get back here tomorrow and read the rest.

Before shutting the book, I turned to the last page on a whim. There was a photograph tucked into the final page with a name scrawled on the back: *Stella Ambrose.*

The faerie in the picture looked somewhat older than me. She had long, dark hair that hung in waves down her back, and she wore a wistful expression on her face. Her wings mesmerized me. They were crystal clear, just like mine. All the faerie wings I'd seen in my life, whether in pictures or now, in person, had been varying colors. Frowning, I flipped back through the book to the richly colored portraits in the *Book of Faerie* to the pages of illustrations of the celebrated Pure Ones. So many pictures. So many wings.

And they were all clear.

21

REVELATION

S omething has changed. I can't quite put my finger on what is different, though I am fairly sure that the One is a she. I've grown weary of waiting and attempt to distract myself.

I flip through the channels on the television in my hotel room, but it's just one inane reality show after another. I have an idea for a show: Wing Hunter, like Survivor for faeries, except that in my version, none survive.

I'VE BEEN positive that the One is in Chapel Hill, but something must be off because she also feels close in Philadelphia. I don't know what that means, which is no small irritation.

At least I've been right about the faerophile. She's been most helpful and will soon be most disposable. I can't kill her quite yet, but it won't be long now. She's told me about an underground club for faeries, so I've added that to my list of places to "visit" when the time is right. the thought of a well-planned inferno gives me great pleasure. They have no idea what's coming for them.

My finger freezes on the remote when I realize what has changed.

She knows what she is.

22

NAKED AND AFRAID

oo tired to read but too stressed to sleep, I tried to calm down. I put the book back in its secret spot but kept the photo. After tucking it into my bag, I decided to try a warm bath. It might be the middle of the night, but I no longer cared about seeming strange to the others. A lighter lay by the side of the tub, so I lit candles around the bathtub and sank into the warm, lavender-scented water.

My wings flattened out behind me against the smooth tub. Wings. If Pure Ones had crystal wings and magical abilities, then what did that make me? I had clear wings, but not even an ounce of magic. Glen was right about me—I really was a freak. More of a freak than anyone could have guessed. As the glow from the flickering candles danced in strange patterns around the dark room, my eyelids grew heavy.

I ZOOMED over the water toward the beach, where faeries frol-

icked in the surf. This time, I knew what was coming. I raced toward them, screaming, "Fly away! He's coming for you!" over and over until my voice was hoarse. The air chilled; he was near. It was the same as before. Faerie after faerie being torn apart by invisible hands—there was nothing I could do to stop it. Then there were none but me. I hovered alone in the dark ocean air. He rushed toward me, but I was powerless to move. As he bore down upon me, I heard a cracking sound. Hot breath whispered, "Lila."

"LILA!"

I sat up, blinking at the bright light of the room. I was still in the bath; chilled water enveloped me, and candle wax ran down the sides of the tub. Ash crouched by the edge of the tub, the door swinging behind him.

"Sorry to bust in, but it's four in the morning, and I heard you yelling. What are you doing taking a bath at this hour?" He looked at me, then averted his eyes.

I glanced down, realizing the bubbles in the bath had long since dissipated. My wings were probably the least interesting body part on display at the moment. I sank lower into the cold water, trying to cover as much as possible with my arms.

"Sorry," I said, blushing. "It was another dream."

"She okay?" Gabriel called out from the hallway.

Great. I'd woken him up. "I'm fine."

Ash reached behind him to grab a towel off the rack. "I just didn't want you to drown or anything. Here, you must be freezing." He handed me the towel, but kept his head turned the other way. "I'll wait in the room for you."

I stood, water cascading off my body, and held the towel across my front. "Ash?"

Hand on the door handle, he turned around. "Yeah?"

"Thanks."

The corner of his mouth went up in his slow smile that made me weak. "No sweat. See you in a minute."

I heard other voices in the hallway, which meant I'd managed to wake up the whole house with my screams, and listened as Ash told them everything was fine and for them to go back to bed. Great—this would really help my hopes of fitting in with this crowd. I tried to shake the images of those dead faeries. Why was it that recurring dreams were always nightmares? I couldn't recall anyone describing recurring dreams about eating chocolate or kissing.

I pulled on my pink sweatpants and one of Corrine's custom T-shirts, then ran my fingers through my damp hair. Going back to the bedroom, I hesitated before walking in the room. After all, Ash was in there, and he'd just seen me totally naked. Mom would so not approve. I took a deep breath and walked in. Ash sat on the edge of his bed.

"Hey," he said, finger-combing his sleep-matted hair.

"Hey, I'm so sorry for all that. If your sister didn't like me before, I'm sure that didn't help." I shut the door and walked over to him.

He patted the bed. "Come talk to me. What's going on?"

Sitting next to him on the bed, I briefly told him about the book.

"So you have the wings of a Pure One but you're not a Pure One?"

I nodded. "I must be some weird hybrid that people don't even know about."

Ash put his arm around me. "I can see why you'd be worried—aside from the serial killer after you, the government would have a field day with you if they knew."

Concern furrowed his brow. "I knew you were one-of-a-kind before tonight. I just didn't realize it was in the literal sense."

I leaned against him. "I don't want to be one-of-a-kind anything. I'm scared to death, and I have no clue how to stop all this."

Ash rubbed my shoulder. "You don't need to figure this out by yourself—we're in it together." He looked me over and flashed a devilish grin. "You look different with clothes on."

I nudged his arm. "Ha, ha."

Ash pulled me close and kissed me, his lips warm on my mouth, my body pressed against his. *I could get lost in him.* The thought made me pull away.

"What is it?" he asked.

I hesitated a second then took a deep breath. "I feel safe when I'm with you but . . ."

"Spit it out."

I sighed. "Well, I have to admit something. I've had a teeny, tiny question as to why all this craziness started happening after I gave you that mint."

Ash nodded. "I've wondered that too. I don't know what it means—but I'm not sorry I met you. You're the best thing that's ever happened to me."

I responded by wrapping my arms around his neck and kissing him. My wings beat faster and faster until I was dizzy. Trying to regain control of myself, I pulled back.

Ash tilted my face toward his. "I want to go as far as you want, Lila . . . if you want."

I gulped. "You mean, like all the way? I don't know . . ."

He nodded. "Okay, I was just thinking . . . if we don't make it out of all this, I'd hate for us to die without knowing what sex was like."

I acted insulted. "What makes you think I don't know

what it's like? Maybe I've had plenty of sex." Ash raised an eyebrow, and I laughed. "Okay, so I don't know what it's like. I am surprised you don't, though."

He shrugged. "I might have had the chance to find out once or twice, but it never felt right. It feels right now, though." He slid next to me on the bed and pulled me close again.

"It may feel right, but not tonight," I said, giving him a quick kiss on the lips. "But I can promise you something."

"What's that?" asked Ash.

I looked into his green eyes. "If we do make it out of this alive—if the killing ends, I promise that I will be more than happy to find out what it's like."

"With me?"

I laughed again. "Of course, with you. How many other guys do you think I've shown my wings to? What kind of girl do you think I am?"

He reached up to touch my wings again. "I think you're a magical girl—and I'm the luckiest guy in the world." He leaned over and kissed me on the neck, lingering long enough for my wings to react. Then he lay back on the bed and patted the empty spot next to him, giving his best slow smile. "I really like you, Lila Rose."

I smiled and crawled into bed, laying my head on his chest. "Back at ya, Ashton . . . hey, what's your middle name?"

Ash laughed. "Don't have one. Just Ash." He kissed the top of my head.

I yawned and stretched my arm across his waist. "Okay, just Ash." The sparkle of my wings dimmed as I became drowsier, drifting toward sleep. Without the light of my wings, the room sank into darkness. Pieces of my nightmare flashed through my mind, intertwined with images of ancient faerie battles. The violent images pulled me under, though I fought to stay awake. Drifting off, I realized there had been a difference in the most recent dream. I'd warned the faeries to get away because *he* was coming for them.

The killer was male.

HOUSE CALL

The faerophile finally contacts me again. Said she doesn't have much time, because they have house guests, and one of them woke everyone up screaming in the middle of the night—said the girl is a faerie. Maybe the girl is simply having run-of-the-mill traumatic dreams due to her kind being slaughtered by yours truly.

But maybe not.

PHOTOGRAPHIC EVIDENCE

The humans in the room didn't notice my anger at breakfast. The faeries sat frozen in place, looking from me to Corrine and back again. They really didn't like me. Ash sat by my side, offering silent support.

"Well?" I demanded. I flashed the photo of the faerie with clear wings at Corrine. "You've all been looking at me like I have three heads. It's because I have clear wings like the Pure Ones and the woman in this picture. Right? What's the deal—you think that I'm like them . . . that I might be planning to overthrow the world with my evilness?"

Corrine cleared her throat. "We don't think you're evil, Lila. We were surprised is all. I was trying to figure out how to tell you."

"Speak for yourself," Jessa coughed under her breath.

I stared at her. "You didn't like me even before you knew what kind of faerie I was."

Jessa didn't blink. "That's true. I don't like outsiders one bit, because they tend to bring trouble. And you're Pure, which means you'll bring even more. And yes, I think apples don't fall far from the tree, so if your ancestors are evil . . ."

"Oh, hush, Jessa." Corrine stamped her foot. "If you can't say something nice, don't say anything at all."

Jessa stood and tossed her long red hair over her shoulder. "Fine. I'm going to study." She stormed off without a look back.

Gabriel whistled. "She has her reasons for being a wench, but I think she was probably that way even before what happened to her sister."

Brooklyn's bright blue eyes focused squarely on me. She looked from me to Corrine. "Corrine, is it really her?"

"I'm right here. I can hear you," I said, annoyed. "Would someone explain this to me?" I gestured at my wings. "If I have wings of a Pure One but not their magic, then what am I?"

"I'm with Lila," said Ash. "I have no idea what's going on but she deserves to know, whatever it is."

"Look at the picture again, honey," Corrine said gently.

I stared at the photo. My eyes moved from the wings to the wistful smile. Yep, she still looked sad. I studied the dark eyes and ebony hair that skimmed her shoulders in barely controlled waves. I smiled. Her hair reminded me of . . . *No way.*

"This is a relative of mine." I stated.

"Yes," said Corrine softly. "Lila, that's your mother."

What? I shook my head. It didn't make any sense. And yet . . . it did. A missing puzzle piece felt like it had clicked into place.

Ash consoled me as tears spilled down my cheeks. *My mother?* Mom had kept many things from me over the years, but this? All these years living together, she never once said, "By the way, sweetie, I'm not your birth mother." Instead, I had to find out miles from home that the person who raised me wasn't my mom. My fingers tightened their grip on the photo. My entire life had been a lie.

"I'm sorry you had to find out this way," said Corrine.

Ash stared wide-eyed at his sister. "This is a huge deal, Corrine. Are you sure?"

I wiped my eyes and nodded. "She's right; now that she said it, it feels right. I know this is my mother." I faced Corrine. "Who is she? Where is she?"

Corrine took a deep breath. "Stella Ambrose, your mother, knocked on our door about two years ago. She had heard about our little commune here and said she needed to hide—that someone was after her. Stella had the most beautiful—and brightest—wings we'd ever seen."

Gabriel nodded. "Like, brighter-than-Vegas-at-midnight bright."

"Stella worried that her being here compromised the safety of the other faeries in the house. She said she wouldn't stay long, and she told us about her daughter."

I reached for Ash's hand.

"Stella had had to leave her daughter with a human to ensure her daughter's survival. She didn't feel it was safe to keep her—she was positive that whoever was after her wanted the baby, too. She cried, saying it wasn't fair that she couldn't raise her own daughter."

I took the tissue Ash offered and blew my nose.

Corrine went on. "Stella said she had made sure to keep her wings bound at all times, so it looked like a normal human pregnancy. She was good friends with one of her neighbors at the time—a woman named Marguerite."

"My mom," I said.

Corrine nodded. "Yes, but she never told us her full name—she was careful not to give any information that she thought would put us in more danger. Anyway, over the course of her pregnancy, she and Marguerite grew very close, and Stella confided in her about being a faerie. Marguerite was the only one she trusted. They agreed that Marguerite would raise the baby. Stella let me take that picture you have there, and I promised I'd keep it. She never saw you again because she didn't want to put you in any danger."

Corrine leaned over and handed me another tissue.

"I can't imagine how hard this is for you to hear," she said, "but I know for a fact that your mother loved you so much that she wasn't willing to risk your life by staying with you."

Ash looked at Corrine as if hesitant to ask the next question. "Corrine, where is Stella? Do you know what happened to her?"

Corrine took a sip of her sweet tea. "All I know is that toward the end of the second week she was here, she started getting real nervous, like she could feel that whoever was after her was getting closer. One morning, we get up, and she's gone. There's just a note on this table saying 'Thanks for everything—I have to keep moving.' We hoped she'd turn up again, but it's been two years, and not a word."

Brooklyn smiled. "But then you show up," she said. "Stella would be so proud to see how beautiful you turned out to be." Brooklyn reached over to touch my wings.

I stared at the picture. *My mother's name is Stella Ambrose.* Lila Ambrose had such a different ring to it than Lila Kincade.

"You keep the picture. It's yours," said Corrine.

Ash leaned over and kissed my cheek. While grateful for the comfort, something still didn't make sense. They kept looking at me like I had three heads. I cleared my throat. "I'm confused about something. The Hiding happened so long ago, but I haven't heard of any faerie murders until recently. So why was someone after her all those years ago? It doesn't seem like it's common knowledge about Pure Ones having clear wings."

Corrine nodded. "There have been other faerie murders ... a bunch happened about ten years ago here in Philly, but the police buried the stories. Then London had a rash of murders just a few months ago—one of them was Jessa's sister. They were also kept under wraps, but I have contacts in the faerie haven cities."

Gabriel chimed in. "And the info about the clear wings was passed on to only a few government officials after the Wars ended. Those officials are the reason the registration laws were created—and strictly enforced. Today, only a handful of high-ranking officials even know about the meaning of wing color."

It turned out that one of those officials was a friend of one of Corrine's connections at the University, a closet faerie-sympathizer. Apparently, wing color was one of the registration questions, although the people who collected the data had no idea about the significance of the answer. The reasoning for this was two-fold. One, they were confident they had gotten rid of all the clear-winged faeries, and two, they didn't want vigilantes trying to take out rogue Pure Ones. I finally understood why Corrine wanted me to keep my wings hidden at the club as a safety precaution.

I bet there had been a third reason, too. My cynical side guessed that if those high-ranking people managed to get their hands on a Pure One, they'd want it kept hush-hush, so they could do all kinds of experiments on them. Maybe that was my paranoia talking, but I had plenty to be paranoid about. Ash grasped my hand tighter, as if he could read my fears.

I wrinkled my brow. "What about everyone who has read *Book of Faerie*? They would know about the wings too."

Gabriel laughed. "Everyone? You mean like the people in this room?"

Brooklyn spoke slowly. "Your mom—Stella—brought it with her. From the faerie realm."

"It's sort of the only copy on Earth," Gabriel added. "Honestly, I think some of the bad Pure Ones who stayed here even after they were ordered to return to their realm didn't think the humans could really kill them—because of their magic.

The only copy on Earth?

Corrine nodded. "Stella's ancestors didn't want those Pure Ones to ever get away with evil again, so they returned to the realm, stole the book, and brought it back to Earth, passing it down from generation to generation."

Brooklyn leaned forward in her chair. She had Jessa's serious demeanor without the attitude. "Think of it as the equivalent of the faerie Bible. Stealing it resulted in the banishment of Stella's entire family from the realm. Stella worried that the Pure Ones might risk coming to Earth to get it back, and when someone started following her, she left it with us for safety. It's yours to take when you want it."

Mine? As much as I wanted the book, it wouldn't be safe with me either, not if a killer was after me. I looked around at the faces around the table. "But I still don't understand the part about my wings. Even if Stella was Pure, my dad was a half-faerie . . . Mom told me so . . ." I stopped, realizing that Mom had probably told me a lot of things that weren't true. "Also, I'm not the least bit magical, so what am I?"

"The wings don't lie, buttercup," said Gabriel. "Your father was Pure—Stella said so herself."

"But . . . but . . . that's impossible," I interjected. "That would make me a . . . a . . ."

"That's right." Corrine beamed at her. "A full-fledged faerie—a Pure One."

25

ANTICIPATION

The One enters the shack, the door creaking on rusty hinges. I wait. She is shaded by the dark of night and I can't see her face. She creeps toward me, a shadowy figure by her side, completely unaware of the horror she will find in this room. It is time. I raise my knife. She screams.

I WAKE from the dream with a smile. I must have fallen asleep in the attic waiting for night, still some hours away. They prattle on below me but I can't discern their idiotic ramblings. I settle back against the wall and put earbuds in and pull up my favorite audiobook, The Necessity of Death: Creating Order From Chaos. it's always good for inspiration in times of doubt. all righteous things require more reserves, and more patience, than we think we can muster. I can admit that I've been impatient, and it has hampered my progress. I am going to do it right this time. Perhaps, someday, there will even be a book written about yours truly and how I saved the fate of humanity.

The faerophile is somewhere downstairs, oblivious that she's led me right to them. I think of my dream and grin—I'm correct *that the One is a girl. That helpful little tidbit narrows down the possibilities. Unfortunately, it will take effort to discover which freak it is, but I'm not concerned. I may know as soon as I see the identity of the mystery houseguest. Content, I close my eyes, place my phone on my lap, and press Play.*

26

PURE AS SNOW

After taking some time to myself in the afternoon and reading more from the library, I finally felt like I had processed most of the information I'd been given. I went outside on the balcony and inhaled the fresh air, comforted by the whispers of the trees around me. Gazing into the vast blue sky above, I marveled at how quickly my identity had changed. One week ago, I was a garden-variety half-faerie whose main concerns included math tests and locker combinations. Now, I was a Pure One, widely thought to be extinct on Earth—and widely hated. For good reason. I tried to wrap my brain around the fact that I was part of the same species that had tried to take over the planet.

Ash took a tentative step out on the balcony. He walked up next to me and followed my gaze to the sky, but then looked quizzically at my wings. "I don't know if it's possible, but your wings are growing brighter by the hour." I glanced behind me: he was right. They sparkled brilliantly in the sunlight.

I stared back at him. "Great. Something else I don't know the reason for."

He placed his hand on the small of my back as Gabriel and Sarah walked out on the balcony. Sarah leaned her head on his shoulder, her blond hair trailing over his black braids.

Gabriel nodded at us. "Guess it's been a hell of a trip, huh?"

I answered with a harsh laugh. "You could say that."

Corrine and Brooklyn joined us a minute later. "Is Jessa still studying?" I couldn't keep the bitterness out of my voice.

"Oh, don't mind her," Brooklyn said. "She needs a boyfriend, if you ask me." Brooklyn's eyes twinkled. She wasn't only less intense than Jessa; she seemed downright friendly.

"Jessa doesn't do well with change," added Corrine. "And you've sort of upturned the apple cart, honey."

I shrugged and turned back to the trees. I couldn't stop wondering what had happened to Stella. Back before the Hiding, the government could only kill Pure Ones after isolating them for long enough to weaken their powers. Pure Ones needed the energy of other faeries to stay strong. Which explained why Stella had to leave me in one of a dozen or so world-wide faerie havens where I'd have plenty of energy to draw from.

I'd read that after the Wars, faeries didn't want all the havens to be in obvious huge cities like New York or Toronto, though they loved London so much, they made it one anyway. They were smart to include a small college town; Chapel Hill was certainly off most people's radar. At least, until now.

The analytic, problem-solving part of my brain couldn't

put it all together, because a) I couldn't feel any energy around me and b) oh yeah, I had no magic powers.

I turned back to the others. "If I'm Pure, wouldn't I know if I was gathering energy from faeries around me? Like when Stella was here, could you tell that she was drawing on your faerie energy—did you feel weaker?"

Gabriel shook his head in unison with the others. "Actually, we all felt stronger when she was here. Same with you here too." He grinned and flexed his bicep. "Hell, I'm always strong, but even more so with a Pure One around."

Brooklyn and Corrine nodded. They felt stronger with me here? Then why wasn't I feeling any different?

"Which brings us to our theory about you," said Brooklyn.

Corrine stepped to the railing. "Someone has been waiting a long time to find you."

"If the dickwad who was after Stella somehow knew she had a child, they'd sure as hell want to track that kid down—even if it took sixteen years," said Gabriel. "Once they guessed it was you, or even narrowed it down, they began taking out as many faeries around you as possible." He crossed his muscled arms over his chest, as if daring someone to try. "Possibly even tried London if they thought it was someone else at first."

I groaned. "Because taking out other faeries would make it easier to kill me."

"Why wouldn't they kill her outright or kidnap her, then take her somewhere isolated until she was weak enough to kill?" asked Ash. He draped his arm protectively around me, like the killer might step out of the trees at any moment.

Brooklyn frowned. "Either they think she has too much power right now to take her or . . . they don't just want to take down the queen but the whole hive."

"Wipe us out entirely," I said, a sinking feeling in my stomach. "If the Pure Ones are gone, taking the half-faeries out will be easy. There wouldn't be any faeries left with enough power to protect them." *But I have no power.* I couldn't save a fly, let alone another faerie.

I thought about the wings I'd seen on eBay, how I'd assumed faeries were being killed for their wings, like elephants for ivory. But a psycho killer wanting to make a buck off faerie wings didn't gel with the calculated and methodical actions of someone who'd tracked Stella for years, and had a more sinister goal of total extinction. Maybe there were two people involved?

"C'mon," said Corrine. "There's fresh sweet tea inside."

My cell phone vibrated as we moved indoors, but I couldn't speak to Mom. What was I supposed to say to her? Even though her reason for keeping the truth from me was due to wanting to protect me—it always was—I couldn't help but feel angry, even betrayed. If it weren't for the love part, I wouldn't have hesitated to give her a piece of my mind. I answered the phone so she wouldn't worry, but only said, "Yes, I'm still fine—I'll call you back later," then hit the End button.

I walked into the living room.

"That your mom?" Ash asked.

I snorted. "It was the woman who told me she was my mother all these years. Not quite the same thing, though."

Corrine squeezed my arm. "I know this is a lot to process, honey. But if Stella trusted Marguerite, then Marguerite is an amazing woman. Besides, any woman who raises you from birth is your mom, whether you like it or not."

I knew she was right, but I didn't want to say it out loud. Instead, I sat down at the table, and Ash rubbed my back while Brooklyn joked about how my wings twinkled at his touch. One of the embarrassing aspects of being unbound was that I wore my emotions on my wings for all to see. The aroma of chicken and brown sugar wafted from the kitchen, where Paul was fixing dinner. The scent reminded me of Mom's recipes, and I couldn't help but smile.

"I hate to bring this up, but we'll have to hit the road right after dinner to get back for school tomorrow." Ash cleared his throat. "If you think it's a good idea to go back at all."

"You're more than welcome to stay here," Corrine added. "In fact, I think it's safer than going home . . . for now, at least."

The analytical math-nerd side of my brain kicked in, concluding that a) faeries were being murdered left and right back home, b) zero faeries had been killed in Philly, and c) I was in Philly so it was safe. So why was my gut screaming at me to go home? It didn't make sense. "I'm leaning toward staying, even though it'll kill my mom. I'll be right back."

I intended to go text Sophie quickly and then leave my phone in the room, but once in the room, I found myself tossing my things in my overnight bag. Why I was packing when I had decided to stay? If I stayed, I could read more of the book—*my* book—and get to know Corrine and the others better.

I set my bag on the bed and noticed Corrine in the doorway, her pink highlights a striking contrast to her pale skin and hair. "Lila, I don't mean to be following you, but if you leave—and I understand if you feel you have to—it was an honor to meet you. We'll always be here."

I have to be alive in order to come back. "Thanks, Corrine. Our ancestry is so amazing, but it's so sad to think about how oppressed we've become." *And how my lineage were the oppressors.*

"Do you want to take the *Book of Faerie* with you now?" she asked.

I shook my head. "Not now. It's safer locked away here. I'll come back for it when this is all resolved."

Corrine flew over and hugged me before heading downstairs. I still couldn't get over just flying whenever you wanted to. She turned back as she left. "Remember the power you have. No one can oppress you unless you let them."

I zipped up the overnight bag. "Really? I'm pretty sure they can force you."

Corrine flashed a high-wattage smile before zipping down the hall. "No, honey. You either fight—or die tryin'."

27

BETRAYAL

"Dinner's ready," said Ash, walking into the room. "I wondered what was taking so long up here. Oh—"

I froze. "What is it?"

He put his hand up. "Don't move. Stay right there, near the window. The way the light catches your wings—it's the most amazing thing I've ever seen."

A sigh of relief escaped me. "I thought something was wrong. I'm glad you're just admiring my unequivocal beauty."

Ash shook his head. "I'm serious, Lila, check yourself out in the mirror behind you."

I turned to examine myself and couldn't help gasping. My wings, which always had a gleam to them, shone like brilliant diamonds. I squinted in defense as I studied them in the mirror. I couldn't remember ever seeing them like this. Maybe it was because they had never been free this long before—they were literally glowing with delight.

"Let's get going, gorgeous," said Ash. He took another

look at my wings, then grabbed his sunglasses and put them on. "That's better."

"Ha, ha. My boyfriend is such a comedian." I couldn't believe the word *boyfriend* came so easily out of my mouth. Almost like I'd had more than one ever.

He kissed me. "I like it when you call me your boyfriend."

"Boyfriend," I said again, and kissed him in return.

THERE WAS a collective intake of breath as we descended the stairs. The sun had started to sink, but light still flooded the west-facing dining room.

Sarah looked in alarm from me to Corrine and back again. "Is that normal?"

Corrine let out a low whistle. "Honey, you could light up the country with those things."

"That's me. The mutant firefly," I muttered.

"You look amazing," said Ash, touching my arm. My wings blazed, and everyone in the room shielded their eyes.

"Holy cow," said Brooklyn. "They were bright last night, but not like this."

"Yeah, like, center of the sun bright," said Gabriel, squinting at me.

"I don't know," I said. "I think they're reveling in their newfound freedom. They've never been unbound for two days in a row before."

Corrine shook her head. "That's not it. We'll figure it out."

"I say we figure it out while we eat. I'm frickin' famished," said Gabriel, bowing his head to shovel food from his plate.

We sat at the long oak table feasting on roasted brown-sugar chicken with sautéed squash and garlic mashed potatoes. There was a comfortable silence in the room. I looked around. "Where's Jessa?"

"Another headache. She's lying down," Brooklyn said, rolling her eyes. She lowered her voice. "Not to be mean, but her attitude sucks."

"Brooklyn," scolded Corrine, but she smiled as she said it. She turned to me. "I wish we knew about your magical ability."

My magic. Right. *I can blind the killer to death with my high-wattage wings.*

Brooklyn rose from the table and paced around the room. "Do you think it could be connected with what's happening with her wings?"

Gabriel shrugged. "We sure as hell can't rule anything out. I just hope we figure it out before the psycho does."

"We will," said Ash. "I'm not letting anything happen to Lila."

I stiffened, biting my tongue. Once again, they were discussing me like I wasn't there.

"I saw something online while I was making dinner," said Paul, nervously tapping his fingers together. "Apparently, due to the murders and continued decrease in the faerie population, faeries have been added to the endangered species list."

"That's great," said Corrine. "A serial killer is out there trying to destroy us, and we get acknowledged as being equivalent to the Sumatran rhino."

Paul shot Corrine a look. "I know it's not enough, but at least they're finally doing something." He coughed. "They also stressed that all faeries in North Carolina should report immediately to the nearest government shelter for their own safety. Maybe you all should consider a shelter as well, since you're associated with . . . Lila."

Corrine rolled her eyes. "Oh right, the Faerie Protection Program. Forgive me if I don't flit over there right away. I mean, they pass all these laws over the years restricting our rights further and further, using all this propaganda crap so people end up hating us more and more. But they don't want to seem like Nazis, so they won't kill us outright." Her eyes flashed with anger. "But I don't believe for one second they give a flying fig about what happens to us."

"Dammit, Corrine," said Paul, hitting his fist on the table. I jumped at the sound. "Is it so strange that I want you and everyone else here alive? That I want you to do what it takes to survive all this?"

Corrine raised an eyebrow at Paul and her voice followed. "By enrolling in the FPP? Are you crazy? Each and every one of those shelters might as well have a sign over it saying 'Kill here.' Plus, they'd register Lila—and the head of the Department of Alternative Human Affairs would know she was Pure. We don't need DAHA involved."

Gabriel sat ramrod straight in his chair, glaring at Paul. "Corrine's right," he said, "the faeries in those shelters are sitting ducks. They're the perfect target for this asshole, and Lila would be up a creek without a paddle."

"Don't you think the government would have extensive security?" asked Paul. "With the number of guards they must have, it would be the safest place for a faerie to be. Please, just think about it, Corrine."

Corrine stood, shaking with anger. "You cannot be that naïve. Trust the government? The same government that has registered us like cattle? That has passed legislation ensuring our eventual demise with their mating laws? Heck, you don't even hear of half-faeries mating with their own kind, because who would want to bring a faerie into this hostile world?" Her voice rose even higher. "Forgive me, Paul, if I don't share your enthusiasm about the ethics and competence of our great leaders. They're feeling cornered because these murders are all over the news. They know how bad it would look if they did nothing, so they're pretending to do something, but it's just an act, Paul."

With that, Corrine stormed out the room, her wings flushing red with anger. Groaning, Paul put his head in his hands, then let out a long sigh and stood. He hesitated as if weighing his options, then walked to the front door.

"Try to understand what we've been through," said Brooklyn softly to him. "It's hard for us to trust humans."

Paul turned to look at her. "I've done nothing but try to understand for the past two years. It would be nice for once if she tried to do the same for me." The door slammed behind him as he left, his tires squealing on the driveway a minute later.

"That was freakin' intense," said Gabriel, before putting another forkful of chicken in his mouth. Next to him, Sarah looked on the verge of tears.

I felt close to a breakdown myself. Maybe I had a power after all—the power to cause disaster.

Ash stood up. "I better go see how my sister's doing."

I nodded absently. Maybe my leaving would make things better for Corrine. School might not be so bad—it's not like someone could kill me in the middle of algebra without being noticed. Besides, hiding hadn't seemed to work out so well for my birth mother, who was always on the run, looking over her shoulder. I was sick and tired of hiding: hiding from my classmates, teachers, even myself. I was done.

"What's going through your head, Lila?" asked Brooklyn.

I bit my bottom lip. "Just weighing my options."

We sat in silence for a bit, and I downed another glass of sweet tea. What I wanted to do was march back into school with my wings out, and though that wasn't possible—or safe—to do yet, it was my long-term goal, assuming I lived that long.

Gabriel swallowed another bite of chicken and gestured with his fork toward my backside. "Any thoughts on your wings, buttercup? I think there's gotta be something to the whole glow-worm thing."

I shrugged.

"I'm interested in your thoughts on that too, honey," said Corrine, walking back into the room with Ash. "Sorry about the outburst. I have a bit of a temper, in case Ash didn't mention it."

"No problem," I said. "I wish I had more of one myself." I tried to rationalize my wing wattage. "As far as my wings go, I thought maybe they were brighter because I'm around all of you . . . you know, taking in energy from my fellow faeries is giving them more power."

Gabriel looked thoughtful, but then shook his head. "That's not it. Sorry to burst your bubble, but that didn't happen with your mom—I mean, Stella."

Corrine nodded. "Any thoughts on how the magic works yet?"

"No." Some all-powerful faerie I turned out to be. I jutted my chin out. "But I've decided that if I'm the only one left of my kind on Earth, I'm going to try to stop this guy, even without magic."

"Don't worry. You'll have all of us at your sides." Ash reached out and rubbed my arm.

My wings blazed again, washing the room in white light.

He removed his hand and my wings returned to a slightly lowered state of gleam.

"Whoa!" said Corrine. She looked deep in thought for a moment, then skittered over to me. She touched my arm, keeping her eyes on my wings. No reaction. Corrine made Brooklyn and Gabriel touch them too. Nada.

"I don't see the point of this," I said.

"Ash, touch her again," said Corrine.

"You don't need to tell me twice." Ash grinned, took his hand and ran the back of it down my shoulder. A blinding light emanated from my wings. He stopped and the light grew dimmer.

"Whoa. That's some cool shit," said Gabriel.

My mind whirled. Ash made my wings brighter, but the others didn't. The only logical difference was that I had strong feelings for Ash, maybe even bordering on—

I bent over and vomited, just as a blood-curdling scream ripped through the house.

28

BACKBONE

"Oh my God, that's Jessa," Brooklyn yelled.

Jessa's screams cut off abruptly, and I ran toward the stairs to help her, but Gabriel grabbed my arm. "Everyone get outside now. I'll check it out." Gabriel gestured toward the back door— and froze.

My gaze followed his. Two police cars sped toward the driveway of the house, their blue-and-red lights flashing, sirens blaring.

Quick footsteps echoed on the floor above, followed by the shattering of glass behind the back of the house.

"What the hell is going on?" Brooklyn asked.

Sarah sobbed uncontrollably.

"Paul. He must have reported us to the DAHA," said Corrine. "I'm guessing he told them there were unregistered faeries living here. He thought he was saving us."

Gabriel stared out at the flashing lights. "Saving us? Your dude is delusional—he totally screwed us. And what just happened upstairs?"

Corrine shook her head. "I don't know."

"Corrine?" asked Ash. "What do you want to do? The police are almost here."

Corrine's eyes focused Ash's keys on the table near the door.

"Run. Fly. All of us. Now!" She grabbed the keys and pushed everyone out the back door toward Ash's truck. The scream of the sirens came close. Sure enough, in the front seat of the first car was Paul. Corrine threw the keys to Ash, telling him to get me to a safe place.

"No, I want to help." I wasn't running away.

"You are helping by going with them." Corrine flew into the air, directly at the cars lining up in front of the house.

When I tried to fly after her, Gabriel grabbed me around the waist and put me in the backseat of Ash's truck, then got in after me so I wouldn't try to jump. Brooklyn hopped in the front passenger seat next to Ash, and Sarah, still sobbing, got in the back with us. Ash gunned the engine and raced through the backyard toward the trees.

We saw Corrine in the rearview mirror, swooping and diving over the police, her voice carrying over the sirens. "Come and get me, suckers!"

"Your sister rocks," said Gabriel. "She blows my mind."

"Yeah, I just hope she doesn't get hurt," said Ash.

"Do you think Jessa's okay?" Sarah sniffled.

No, I wanted to scream at her, *I'm pretty sure she's freakin' dead*. No, I wasn't pretty sure. She was dead. I knew it in my gut.

Gabriel punched the seat. "Was that psycho in our house? If I'd gotten my hands on him—"

"You'd be dead," I finished. "The cops saved us, in a way. They scared him off."

"Yeah, right. You can't kill this." Gabriel flexed his bicep.

I didn't know how to explain to them what my gut was

telling me, because it wasn't logical or rational, but I knew that if the cops hadn't arrived, most—if not all—of us would be dead by now. As strong as Gabriel was, it wouldn't have been enough. And I couldn't have lifted a finger to stop it because I. Had. No. Magic.

Gabriel surveyed the road ahead. "Stay on this dirt road. It dumps you out onto the main road up ahead."

Low-hanging branches scraped the sides of the truck as we zoomed through the trees. Ash didn't let up on the gas.

I gripped the seat. "I should have helped Corrine."

Brooklyn shook her head. "I'm sure Corrine will join us soon. You need time to figure out some things. You'll have more power if Gabriel and I are with you."

Ash slowed down as we approached the main road.

Gabriel jerked his head around. "I don't see any cops. You're good to go."

Ash pulled out into traffic. Tense silence filled the truck. I couldn't help scanning the trees, hoping for a glimpse of rose-colored wings.

Sarah sat rigidly, pressed against the door. I wanted to comfort her but didn't know of anything especially comforting to say. Instead, I nudged Gabriel and jerked my chin toward Sarah.

"Sarah?" asked Gabriel. "You okay?"

Sarah started crying all over again. "No, I'm not. I don't know where you guys are going, but I can't leave school right now. My parents would kill me. I . . . I didn't know things were going to get so complicated. I can't handle this."

Gabriel's jaw clenched. "It's okay, Sarah. Do you want us to drop you off?"

Sarah nodded, tears streaming down her face. "I'm so sorry, Gabriel. It's not that I don't want to be there for you. I don't want to break up or anything."

"Yeah, okay, we can talk about it later. Ash, can you pull over?" asked Gabriel.

"Here on the side of the road?" Ash asked.

"Yes please," said Sarah between sobs. "I'll call my folks to get me."

My heart broke for both of them, but I didn't know how to fix it. Ash pulled over, and Sarah climbed out, still sobbing. "Call me," she said through her tears. "And I'm sorry ... for ... a lot of things—"

"Whatever. We gotta jet, Sarah. Sorry," said Gabriel, as he slammed the door shut. "Go, Ash."

The car sped away from the curb. "It doesn't sound like you're going to call her, big guy," noted Brooklyn. "You've been together, what, like three years? Aren't you being a tad harsh?"

"It's been a great three years," said Gabriel, stone-faced. "But it's a tough gig being with a faerie. That means if you're gonna be with one, you have to do it all the way. There's no room for half-assed stuff."

"Sorry, man," said Ash. He glanced in the rearview mirror at me and his look said everything.

I smiled despite the adrenaline still coursing through my veins.

"Do you think Corrine got away?" asked Brooklyn when we stopped at a red light.

"If anyone could, it'd be Corrine," said Gabriel.

Brooklyn nodded, but Ash's face was grim, his lips pressed together. He focused intently on the road in front of him. After a few moments of silence, he glanced in the rearview mirror and groaned. "By the way, you might want to try to figure out a way to keep your wings under wraps. Especially you, Lila. You look like a giant sun-catcher."

In all the chaos of escaping the police, I'd forgotten

about my wings. I was sitting in a car in broad daylight, my wings reflecting each and every drop of sunshine. I hunched down, trying to flatten them against the seat.

Gabriel opened a compartment in the backseat and, after digging around for a minute, held up binding material and tape. "Corrine's motto is 'always be prepared.' We've got food, water, a first aid kit. And"—Gabriel pulled out a crow bar—"a back-up plan." He looked at the binding material then winked at me. "You first, buttercup."

I blushed, still not used to the hot-guy-faerie thing. "Right," I said, brushing my hair from my neck and turning my back toward Gabriel. Sadness swept through me as my wings were pushed back against my body and covered with the heavy fabric. *Sorry, girls*, I thought. *It's been fun.* My wings fluttered in protest, then fell limply against my back in resignation.

"We have to figure out somewhere safe we can take you. Then we'll wait for Corrine to text us so she can find us," said Ash.

"We should keep Lila near as many faeries as possible," said Brooklyn. "What about the faerie colony in downtown Philly?"

"Well, it's close, but she needs to be farther away from that psycho. I'm thinking London," said Gabriel. "He'd prob-ably assume she'd be at an East Coast spot."

I stayed silent. Didn't they realize I'd never get away from the killer? He'd follow me to London, just like he had to Philly. How did he keep finding me? It was like the dreams I'd had as a little girl, where I would run through fields, rooms, and buildings, yet my murderous dream killer would find me seconds later. Enough damage had been done on my account. There was no running away from this guy. I was going to face him where I was most comfortable—at home.

Brooklyn chewed on her nail, lost in thought. "Yeah, overseas might work. London has the largest colony of all."

"Or *had* anyway," Gabriel noted. "Before the killings this summer."

I wanted to cry and laugh at the same time. They were talking about trans-Atlantic travel, and I hadn't been more than fifty miles from home before this weekend.

"Do you have a preference, Lila?" asked Ash, glancing back at me in the mirror.

"I'm not going anywhere except home," I announced.

He frowned. "Lila, I know you miss your mom, but we're trying to save your life here."

"Save my life? You're sounding an awful lot like Paul right now."

The car grew dead quiet and my cheeks grew hot. I'd hurt his feelings. I reached up from the back seat, touching his shoulder. "I'm sorry, I didn't mean that. Look, I know I'm safest around other faeries, but you guys said it yourselves— Chapel Hill is a faerie colony too."

"I don't know," said Ash. Brooklyn braced as if expecting another replay of the fight between Corrine and Paul. But I wasn't Corrine, and Ash definitely wasn't Paul.

"Please," I said, "I'll be safer at school than anywhere else. I don't want him to think that I'm afraid, and maybe I can help other faeries in the area."

"But buttercup," said Gabriel, "it's not just the psycho I'm worried about. Won't school be the first place the cops look for you? Paul knows what school you go to."

Ash shook his head. "I don't think Paul would ever tell them that."

"How do you know?" Brooklyn asked.

"He loves Corrine and wanted to keep her safe. He probably came with the police to try and reason with her about going to a shelter, which I'm sure did not go over well," said Ash. I smiled, thinking of how Corrine must have reacted when Paul stepped out of the car, asking her to fly down and talk to the police. That would not have been a quiet conversation.

"Anyway," said Ash. "Paul is all about Corrine. I don't think he had an interest in getting everyone else in trouble or ratting anyone out for being unregistered. Once Corrine talks to the officers, I hope they'll let her go."

"I hope you're right," said Gabriel, "because Paul knows what Lila is. What if he feels it's his duty to inform the government that a Pure One exists? They'd track her down for sure."

"Ugh." I shuddered. "It's like one of those movies where they decide to 'experiment' on the alien life form. I really don't want to end up in some government lab with my wings pinned to a board." A nagging thought tugged at my mind. If the killer was the same person who put wings in my locker and followed me to Philly, did that mean he already knew I was more than a regular faerie?

I turned to Gabriel. "The killer was in the house with us. Do you think he overheard us talking about my being Pure?"

Gabriel and Brooklyn exchanged glances. She shrugged. "I'm not sure, but even if he doesn't know you're Pure, I'm guessing he suspects it."

Gabriel nodded. "I agree. He had plenty of half-faeries to kill in your area, but he dropped everything to follow you here. Are you sure you still want to go home?"

"Yep." I didn't hesitate. "Plus, one of my teachers is a faerie too, and I bet there are others."

"What? Who?" Ash asked.

"Mr. Finch. I meant to tell you. At least I'll be safe in his class."

"That's wild," said Ash. "I had no idea."

"Yeah, anyway, I better text Mom and let her know we're coming. She and I have a long talk ahead of us." I hesitated a moment, my fingers hovering over my phone.

Ash glanced at me in the mirror. "Don't be too hard on her. Your mom has done everything she thought she had to do to keep you safe. Stella trusted her with your life, so that should count for something."

"I know. It's just that she takes overprotectiveness to a whole new level."

Ash shrugged. "That's sort of the job description. So, Chapel Hill it is."

I cracked the window. The crisp fall breeze blew across my face and lifted my hair. It was the closest thing to flying I could imagine. Burnt orange leaves tumbled in the wind, and I envied them as they danced in the air around the trees. *I can't believe I'm jealous of a leaf.*

Brooklyn seemed to read my thoughts. "I can't wait until we can fly freely. Just up and go whenever we feel like it."

"It doesn't look like that'll happen in this lifetime," said Gabriel. He cracked his knuckles. "Any word from your big sis, Ash?"

Ash double-checked his phone. "Not yet."

We took turns driving throughout the evening, the sky darkening around us, the air damp, and the night quiet now that the cicadas of summer were gone. I was happiest when it was Gabriel or Brooklyn's turn to drive, so I could cuddle with Ash in the backseat. I leaned my head on his shoulder and dozed off as miles of highway went past in a blur. I could almost sense it as we crossed into Orange County—the air grew thicker. The sky looked the color of black ink by the time we turned onto my street, but my house was a homing beacon. Every room appeared to be lit. Mrs. Nesbaum's house was black save for a dim porch light out front. I'd barely stepped out of the car when Mom tore out of the house into the driveway, hugging me close and crying.

"Oh, baby, I've been so worried about you," she sobbed through her words. "Don't you ever do anything like that again or you're grounded for life. And I'm not happy with anyone who participated in this." Mom glared at the group behind me.

"Don't be mad at anyone else," I said. "I made Ash take me there."

"Hmmph. I haven't decided about that yet," Mom said, hugging me again.

"Well, I have some people I want you to meet, so be nice." I introduced Brooklyn and Gabriel to Mom, then glanced next door. "Is Mrs. Nesbaum okay? Her house is totally dark. She always sleeps with all the lights on."

Mom wiped the remaining tears from her cheek and glanced toward our neighbor's house. "I thought they were on earlier. I'll call her in a little bit to check on her."

Ash and I helped Mom whip up a midnight spread of spaghetti, salad, and garlic bread for everyone. We gave a brief account of the events in Philadelphia, skipping the murder part for now. I unzipped my bag and brought out the photo.

"Oh, by the way . . . do you recognize her?" I flipped the picture in front of her face.

She gasped and spoke in a halting voice. "Lila—"

I held up my hand. "It's okay, Mom. I've done a lot of thinking while we were driving. I realize you sacrificed your entire life to raise another woman's child, and I owe every-thing to you." I smiled at her. "Plus, you never did seem the type to have some crazy affair."

"Thanks, I think." Mom stood to fetch seconds for Gabriel. "Oh, look, Mrs. Nesbaum's lights are on again. There she is in the window. What is she doing up at this hour?" We watched Mrs. Nesbaum putter around her kitchen for a minute.

Turning back to the table, I remembered all the times Mom and I had sat at this very table, talking. Just the two of us. All the nights Mom never once went out on a date, despite the offers. For me. To keep me safe at all costs. I jumped out of my chair and into her arms, giving her a fierce embrace.

Mom said that Brooklyn and Gabriel could stay at our house, with Brooklyn in my room and Gabriel on the living room couch. Mom seemed relieved to have the support. She said there was no way on earth we were going to school on Monday, being that it was already well past midnight, and she really preferred I not go at all. After arguing awhile, we decided to try school on Tuesday, with *try* being the operative word.

Ash would meet us here each day, and we'd go to school in Ash's truck, where Gabriel would drop us off—no more walking. I wasn't sure how I'd explain it to Sophie, but I needed time to come up with something better than *Sorry I can't walk with you to school anymore, but I'm a faerie with a serial killer after me.*

Brooklyn called her mother, who would enroll her at Northeast High in the morning. Although she was a college sophomore, Brooklyn easily looked young enough to pass for a high school student. Brooklyn's mom would say that Brooklyn was my cousin and would be living with the Kincades for a time. I was relieved to know that faeries would be with me at all times. But even though I felt safer, I was afraid I was putting them in harm's way all the same.

Ash stretched his arms. "I'm going to have to take off here in a minute to get home to my mom. She's been worried sick." He checked his phone again. "I really wish Corrine would call."

"Hey, flip on the news a sec before you go," said Gabriel. "Maybe there's something about a police standoff in Philly."

"No, it's late," I said, racing for the remote, but Mom had already flicked on the TV. If there was anything on the news about a faerie murder in Philly, I'd be under lock and key. The panic must have shown on my face, as Gabriel mouthed "sorry" to me. The anchorwoman reported no new leads in the recent faerie murders, and didn't report any new murders. We looked at each other questioningly. Could Jessa be alive? Then the woman stated that in other faerie news, an unregistered faerie had been captured.

The scene cut to an earnest-looking man sporting a headset. He reiterated that being unregistered was a serious crime, and emphasized that unregistered faeries tended to be the most dangerous, as proven by an unfortunate incident involving a faerie in Philadelphia. Descriptions included "hostility toward the peacekeeping officers" and "aggressive tendencies that warranted the use of a Taser." He even had the nerve to repeat that horrid commercial. Gazing into the camera, he said, "Remember folks, unregistered equals unsafe." So registered faeries were welcome at the local FPP shelter, but unregistered ones would have stiff penalties to pay—whether they had a serial killer after them or not.

I looked at the background and focused on the street where the reporter stood. There wasn't a picture of the offending faerie, but I didn't need one. The reporter went on to say that the unregistered faerie had been arrested and detained. Corrine was in jail.

REGRETS

I haven't been this aggravated in a long time. To be so close to the goal, only to have it ripped away . . . After taking out the easy target, the rest were all ripe for the picking. It should have been so simple. Only a flight of stairs between me and a roomful of freaks and faerophiles. The loud, opinionated girl had been the only one I heard from upstairs, and she wasn't the One.

The police . . . oh, the damn police. Don't they realize I'm helping them? All these years, they haven't cared about faeries dying, as long as they were the ones killing them. But as soon as someone else steps in to lend a hand, they act like killing vermin is a crime. Hypocrites.

Perhaps I should have waited to kill the roommate, but sometimes my emotions get the best of me. She had some lungs on her, that one did. If only I had been able to hear the rest of them screaming in symphony.

I need to get home, so I can get back to the business at hand. My sensing the One here seems to be an error, though I'd been so sure. When I do find her, I'll take my time. She is really starting to piss me off.

MISSING

I zipped across the ocean while faeries danced along the shoreline.

I knew this dream. Darkness was about to fall, and the bloodbath would begin at any moment. I hated this dream.

Although my warnings would be futile, I cried out to them anyway. But this time, as the shadow crossed the water and faeries fell around me, a new sound emerged behind their desperate screams. It was a steady sound that grew louder and louder, but it came from another direction. I turned around, but I couldn't see anything behind me. The faerie killer was looming toward me, and was almost upon me. The sound thundered in my ears behind me, ever closer. It was someone else—they were coming to help me. It took a moment longer to recognize the sound, but then it was crystal clear. It was the beating of wings.

THE ALARM WENT OFF TUESDAY, bringing me out of one nightmare and into another. I was going to school, back to the place where a murderer was stalking me. Maybe he would interpret my actions as bold, and wouldn't guess the fear that ran from the bottom of my feet to the tips of my wings. I engaged the problem-solving side of my brain, but I couldn't figure out the killer's next move. *Maybe because I'm not psychotic like him.* Even knowing I'd see Ash did little to steady my nerves.

"We can always leave," said Brooklyn. "Really, if it gets bad, we'll just take off with the others and go into hiding. Or maybe we can try to bust Corrine out of the shelter."

I cracked a smile. I almost felt sorry for the shelter workers. They were sure to be getting an earful from the defiant, pink-haired faerie—if she hadn't found a way to escape already.

"I can hear her now," said Brooklyn. She tossed her hair back in Corrine fashion and glanced at me in mock scorn. "You're supposed to be protecting us and you Tasered me? I hope you've got good lawyers because I'm suing your asses as soon as I get out of here. What's next, 'protective' electroshock therapy?"

I doubled over with laughter, thinking maybe Corrine would be released just so they could have some peace and quiet.

"I'm glad you're finding some humor in this situation. I wish I could."

I turned to find Mom in the doorway, waiting with tape to bind our wings.

"Oh, hi, Mom. Just a little black humor to take the edge off things."

My wings did not bend easily against my back; they seemed angrier than usual at their containment. In between each carefully placed strip of tape came another warning from Mom, another plea to come home if I felt uncomfortable, another reminder to call 911 from my cell phone if needed. After what happened with Corrine, the police would be the last people I'd call.

ASH KEPT quiet the whole way to school. At my locker, I wordlessly took his hand in mine. I didn't want to push him to talk. He leaned his head against my locker, staring at me. Despite his sadness, my wings fluttered against their bindings under his gaze.

"Hey," he said at last.

"Hey, yourself," I said. "I'm sure Corrine will be fine. Don't worry."

He sighed. "Yeah. I just want to hear from her." He looked tired and drained. "I missed sleeping with you last night."

I glanced over at Brooklyn. "He didn't mean it like that. We just slept in the same bed."

Brooklyn laughed. "It's none of my business what you kids do. When I was your age . . . oops, I better not say that too loud. I'm supposed to be sixteen, after all."

I frowned. "If your mom had to fax your records and stuff, won't your birth date be on there?"

"You don't know my mom. I'm one of the 'unregistered' varieties. She doesn't trust many people, especially the government and their anti-mating laws. She'll figure out a way to send the school what they need, even if it's not totally accurate."

Ash looked impressed. "There must be a lot of unregistereds out there. Is Gabriel unregistered too?"

Brooklyn shook her head. "No, he and his dad are registered. His dad is pretty conventional; they do everything by the book."

"Lila! Where have you been? You must have been

really sick. Are you better?" Sophie ran up to me then stopped in her tracks when she saw Brooklyn. "Who are you?"

I explained about her being my out-of-state cousin who was living with us.

Sophie frowned. "You never mentioned anything about having a cousin." Her eyes widened like she just figured something out and her brow darkened. "Oh, I get it. Not so sick, huh? Just found something better to do." Sophie looked more than a little hurt as she turned and stormed off down the hall. Clearly, she thought I'd been blowing her off. If I made it through everything, I was going to tell her the truth no matter what the consequences.

The early bell rang and students began filing in, bringing the hallway to life.

Ash stepped up to me. "Don't worry about her. You can make it right later. You and Brooklyn better get to the office to get her schedule." He wrapped his arm around my waist. "You be careful—I'll be waiting in first period for you. If anything happens, call my cell. Promise."

"I promise," I said. I put my hands on his face and pulled him to me so I could kiss him in a way that school personnel would label inappropriate. His kiss was worth a detention —or ten.

Brooklyn cleared her throat. "Can this wait until later?"

I forced myself to pull away from him. He flashed me a weak smile. "I'm liking this new side of you."

I blew him a kiss and went with Brooklyn to Mr. Turner's office. Ms. Gable was sitting near his desk chatting with him when I knocked on the open door.

"Hi Mr. Turner, Ms. Gable."

"Lila, it's nice to see you. This must be Brooklyn," said Mr. Turner, offering his hand. "Brooklyn, I spoke with your mother earlier this morning. I'm so sorry to hear about . . . your situation."

Brooklyn knew her mother had given a vague account of a traumatic incident that necessitated her move to my house. Her mother also strongly suggested that she be in all my classes in order for her to have additional support. Tears cascaded down Brooklyn's face, and I played along, putting my arm around my "cousin" in an attempt to console her while they sorted out her schedule.

Mr. Turner watched us with grave expressions and began filling out paperwork for Brooklyn, including an immediate referral to the school psychologist. I looked up, surprised to see that Ms. Gable was still in the room, looking at us with narrowed eyes. I gulped. What would happen if Ms. Gable accused us of lying? Ms. Gable opened her mouth to speak, shut it, then opened it again.

"Well, girls," she said as she stood. "I guess this means you both have my class first this morning. I might as well escort you there."

I breathed a sigh of relief. Brooklyn gave me a quick wink as they followed Ms. Gable to the door.

"Oh, Ann—er, Ms. Gable," Mr. Turner called out. She turned with a questioning look on her face.

"That dish sounds terrific. Stop by later and we can set up a time."

Ms. Gable walked the entire way to her classroom with a smile plastered across her plump face.

My relief at having Brooklyn near turned to fear within seconds.

Ash's seat was empty.

31

THE OTHER SIDE OF NORMAL

F ive minutes passed. Then five more. Ash still wasn't there. My fingers inched toward my backpack, where my phone was. Texting in class was forbidden, but I couldn't stand much more waiting. My panic rose from moderate distress to near full-blown hysteria. Brooklyn stared at me wide-eyed. My pencil sat unused on the desk, while the class worked on useless equations.

Ms. Gable came up and whispered, "Are you okay, Lila?"

If feeling like I would vomit any second equaled okay, then I was doing fabulous. "I'm okay. Just tired."

The door to the class opened and thirty heads swiveled around.

Ash walked in, and his eyes connected with mine. I didn't realize my sigh of relief was so audible until the heads swiveled back to me like in a tennis match. He nodded briefly, then took his seat in the back of the room.

"Everything okay here?" Ms. Gable tapped her pen on the desk.

Ash responded to Ms. Gable's question but held my eyes as he answered it. "Yeah, everything's okay."

I turned around to face the front of the room. Something big had happened—big enough that he was late for class. But he was here; that was the important thing.

Seconds ticked by, one, by one, by one. Class lasted an eternity. Ash was only a few feet away from me, yet he might as well have been in another dimension. There were still ten minutes of class left, but I needed to talk to him *now*. I never thought I'd see the day when I'd want algebra to end early, but here it was. I willed the bell to ring early.

The bell rang.

"That's strange," said Ms. Gable. "The period doesn't end for another ten minutes." Her comments fell on deaf ears as students scrambled out the door.

I ran to Ash and threw my arms around him, not caring about the display of affection in front of Ms. Gable. Ash glanced at her, and pulled Brooklyn and me toward the hallway. I fixated on Ash, but could have sworn I heard Ms. Gable call out "Be careful" as we left the room.

"Holy hell, I almost had a coronary when you weren't in class. What's going on?" I asked, not taking my hand off Ash's arm.

"I got a text from Corrine. So I hung out in the bathroom."

I threw my arms around Ash. "She's alive! Is she okay? What happened?"

"Like we thought, the cops came because Paul told them Corrine should be in a shelter. He thought it would somehow protect her if she was on the police radar, but of course, they found out she was unregistered. Her original charge was for the unregistered part, but disturbing the peace and resisting arrest added to the list."

"And?" Brooklyn asked.

"Some of her connections at the University pulled

strings to get her released this morning, after an evaluation by a psychologist to make sure she wasn't 'dangerous.'"

I laughed and exhaled a sigh of relief. "So, where is she?"

Ash swallowed. "You know her. She's coming here to help, of course. She didn't want to wait for anyone to come get her. I tried to talk her out of it but she wouldn't hear of it. Said she'll stick to the woods so she can fly as much as possible without being seen—it's the fastest way. She'll call when she's near."

"I can't wait to see her," said Brooklyn. "Did Paul tell the police anything else?"

"Just that Corrine and 'other faeries' lived together at that house. He didn't say anything about Lila, and he said he realized reporting Corrine was the wrong decision."

"Did she forgive him?" I asked.

"Of course not; she's Corrine."

The school bell rang. "How are we supposed to sit through these classes?" I asked. "Acidity levels, Shakespeare, and algebraic equations don't hold a candle to death and dismemberment. I can't concentrate."

"Well, let's at least go to class. We don't want to annoy Birchester again," said Ash.

Brooklyn was given a brief introduction to the class. My lab partner, Jacinda, smiled at me, and I couldn't wait to expose my true self without fear of repercussions. *Can't we all just get along?* I looked out the window at a tree swaying in the wind, and the familiar yearning started in my wings. Sophie refused to even look my way. She had every right to be mad at me, but I hated that we weren't speaking. She wasn't even responding to my texts.

Jacinda's counting of electrons jerked me back to the classroom. I stared at the four white walls and low ceiling, feeling suddenly claustrophobic. It was like being trapped in a box. Would I ever feel free again like I had that day in my backyard when I was five?

Jacinda yawned. "This is straight-up boring. Hey, are you goin' to Fall Formal? Jake asked me over the weekend."

"I don't know," I said, knowing how lame that sounded. It wasn't like going to a dance had ever been an option. A formal dress wouldn't conceal what I needed it to. Although my everyday clothing would best be characterized as dorky, showing up to a dance in a baggy dress would be fashion suicide. Anyway, it was hard to think about normal things like a school dance when I wasn't sure I would live through the end of the day.

Jacinda rolled her eyes. "Give me a break, girl. Ash's hotter than hot. What? Don't act all surprised—everybody knows he's into you. That boy's been stuck to you like Elmer's."

"Maybe. I'll think about it," I muttered. I peeked over at Brooklyn, who was working diligently at her station, apparently quite attentive to her lab partner, Dylan. Ash must have noticed too, because when I turned around, he nodded his head in Brooklyn's direction and smirked.

After class, Ash took a jab at Brooklyn. "I see you're really playing the part of the eager high school student. It's good it's just an act, 'cause Dylan's a little young for you, you know?"

A flush crept across Brooklyn 's face. "I was just being friendly. I *am* new here, you know. Plus, I'm two years younger than Corrine, you know."

"No need to be defensive. I was making an innocent observation is all," said Ash.

I laughed as Brooklyn glared at both of us. It felt almost like a normal school day.

"It's good to see you smiling again, Lila. Last time I saw

you, you were pretty upset," said a voice behind me.

I spun around. "Oh, thanks, Mr. Finch. See you in class." Upset wasn't even the word for the train wreck I'd been in front of his class. Though now I wished I could stay in his class all day. The more faeries, the better.

"Looking forward to it," he said, as we made our way through throngs of students toward our lockers.

"Hello, fair maiden," Curtis called as he strode past in a hurry.

Ash cocked his head toward me. "I think that guy has a little crush on you."

I scoffed. "Don't be silly; he's just nice. By the way, did you hear about Fall Formal?" I just wanted to see what he'd say.

Ash flashed that sexy grin of his. "I've been meaning to talk to you about that. I've decided that if we all make it through this, you're going to the dance with me."

"You've decided, huh? Well, I have a strange feeling that one way or another, this thing will be over by then, and if I'm still alive, I wanna dance." Maybe I could wear a shawl over my dress.

We linked hands, and Ash teased Brooklyn. "Brooklyn could rob the cradle and ask Dylan."

Brooklyn gave him a playful punch on the arm. My skin prickled, and I turned and braced myself when I saw Glen striding toward us—except he didn't walk up to me. Instead, he got in Ash's face and pointed his finger at him. "You're seriously pickin' the freak over Luscious Lexie? Dude, maybe it's time to re-evaluate your girlfriend criteria."

Ash surveyed Glen calmly. "She's not a freak, and if you don't walk away right now, you're gonna be in a world of hurt."

Glen took a step back and held his hands in mock

surrender. "I'm just sayin'—it would suck being the new kid if everyone thought you were hanging with freaks."

Ash studied him. "Come up to me—or call Lila a freak again, and see what happens. I dare you."

Glen shrugged but didn't say anything else before walking away.

Ash turned to Lila. "Sorry about that. I don't normally condone violence."

Brooklyn looked horrified. "Who was that, and why does he hate you?"

"I wish I knew," I said. "As far as I can tell, it's because I'm good at math, and he's friends with someone who thinks I'm a lame dresser."

Brooklyn stared after him. "What a creep."

"You can say that again," said Ash. "He comes near you again, you tell me."

I nodded as I dialed my locker combination. Memories of the grotesque picture made me catch my breath. I swung open the locker, not sure what to expect. There was nothing. No news clippings, no photos. My shoulders relaxed.

"Hey, y'all," said Jacinda, heading toward us, her dark curls bouncing in a ponytail. "My parents are out of town this weekend so we're having a little par-tay at my place Friday. Hope you can make it."

Jacinda addressed her next comment to Brooklyn. "Oh, Dylan mentioned to me that he'll *definitely* be there. Just sayin'."

"Why are you telling me?" said Brooklyn, her cheeks pink.

"Oh, he just might've mentioned to me that he thought you were cute," said Jacinda.

Ash snorted, and Brooklyn scowled at him. I chuckled, grateful for Jacinda and her invitation. Grateful for this amazing boy and for Brooklyn. Were these the things normal teenagers experienced? It seemed unfair that by sheer virtue of possessing a few extra parts, I was forever banned from the world of normal.

"Thanks, Jacinda," I said. "We'd love to come."

"Great, see you then," said Jacinda.

Ash stared at me in shock. I frowned. "What? Why are you looking at me like that?"

"Are you on crack?" he asked. "A serial killer is after you, and you've decided the best way to handle it is to go to a party? A party your mother would never allow you to go to?"

My face fell. "Look, I want to feel normal for a change. I'm sick of always doing the safe thing."

He sighed. "I hear you, Lila, but this probably isn't the best time to declare your emancipation to the world."

We argued all the way to next period, attempting to keep our voices down to avoid attention. By lunch, we were both so exhausted from fighting that we fell into a resigned silence. It wasn't fun, but at least nobody had tried to kill me. In fact, the worst thing that happened was Finch assigning us a new essay.

"Well, I guess that rules out the party. We'll have to plan a study date instead." The hope in Ash's voice was unmistakable.

I made a face at him. "Sure, whatever."

"Yeah, I'm not really into the whole high school homework thing again—I hope the killer is found before midterms, or I'm going to have serious issues," Brooklyn said.

I studied Brooklyn as she grabbed the books from her locker at the end of the day and stuffed them in her backpack. "What are you going to do about the fact that you left school mid-semester? Isn't that a big deal?"

Brooklyn shrugged. "If things aren't resolved in a few weeks, Corrine will be able to pull some strings with her friends in the administration."

I dropped my bag and bent over, gagging as a sudden wave of nausea overcame me. What was with my stomach? It was hard to look brave when I felt like hurling at random moments.

Brooklyn's eyes widened. "Lila, are you okay?"

"My stomach feels like a cement mixer," I said.

Ash helped me up and retrieved my books. Brooklyn rubbed my back until the feeling passed.

"I'm good now," I said weakly.

Ash and Brooklyn remained on either side, as though uncertain whether to believe me.

"I'm fine. I mean it. Let's get going," I said in a mock-cheerful voice.

Ash hesitated, then linked his hand with mine. We headed outside to wait for Gabriel.

I was excited for Gabriel to hear the good news about Corrine. I glanced over my shoulder to make sure I wasn't missing something. There had been no grotesque pictures in my locker, no creepy notes, no nothing. It would have been easy to pretend this was a normal day at school, but I was wary of letting myself be lulled into a false sense of safety.

In the parking lot, I stared at the wooded area surrounding the school. A hint of a breeze stirred the dense air. The leaves about to change from green to gold and red. It was a beautiful fall day—nothing out of the ordinary. But I sensed it. The hairs of my neck stood on end.

Right at this moment, from the direction of the woods, someone was watching me.

32

PREDATOR AND PREY

So close now, I can almost smell her. A key piece just fell into my lap, literally, though not willingly, and none too soon. I cannot believe my good fortune. It's as though the universe itself is aligned with my plan, and has offered up divine intervention. In even more good news, I hear there's a big party on Friday. I'm so hoping she attends. She may have the benefit of magic, but I have the advantage of conviction.

THIS IS GOING to be a weekend to end all weekends.

33

THE DEVIL YOU KNOW

I spooned rice onto plates while Mom served her favorite baked chicken recipe. I inhaled the scent of the comfort food, grateful to be surrounded by friends. With the blinds closed tight, we faeries displayed our wings with pride. Mom stared at mine, then at the others' and back to mine again. I realized in that glance that she didn't know what I was. Stella had kept some secrets, even from her. How would I even begin explaining that I was Pure?

After dinner, I dished out brownies and ice cream. Gabriel was thrilled to hear about Corrine, and we laughed at Ash's accounts of her incarceration. As the hours passed into late evening and we'd long since finished dessert, Ash turned somber. He was worried.

"How fast can faeries fly?" I asked. "It's sad that I don't know, but it's not like I've flown much."

Ash glanced at his phone, checking the messages. "Fast. She tested herself once, and hit 120 miles per hour."

"I've hit 140," said Gabriel with a shrug in my direction. "There's no bird alive faster than a faerie, buttercup. Magic blows the whole wingspan physics of Earth out of the water."

My mouth fell open. "Wow, I had no idea." With a sinking feeling, I realized that meant Corrine should have been here by now.

Ash pushed his plate away and stood. "I better get home. My mom is probably freaking out."

I walked him to the door and looked into his eyes. There was something there I'd never seen before: fear. Even with everything that had happened so far, he'd seemed confident things would turn out okay. He didn't look confident right now.

"Look," I said, "I don't know why Corrine isn't here yet, but I do know that if anyone could make it, it's her. I've never met a stronger person, or faerie, in my entire life." I kissed him lightly on the lips. "Promise me you'll call me as soon as you hear anything?"

He nodded but seemed distracted. His shoulders were slouched as he walked to his truck.

After they left, Brooklyn paced back and forth across the first floor of the house. "Something's wrong . . . I know it. Corrine would have flown through fire to get to Ash."

My own anxiety spiked with every lap Brooklyn did through the living room, and my fear grew with every muttered comment that dropped from her lips. At last, Mom whispered in Brooklyn's ear, and Brooklyn disappeared up the stairs. Although fainter, her quick footsteps could still be heard pacing around the bedroom.

"Lila, I'm so sorry about Corrine. I hope everything is okay—for Ash's sake. For everyone's sake," Mom said. "Can you sit down for a minute, sweetie?"

I hadn't realized that I too had been walking in circles. Gabriel excused himself, saying he was already in need of leftovers. I plopped down in one of the plush living room chairs, my phone by my side. Mom left the room and returned a minute later. She pushed a photograph into my hand. I looked down at my biological mother, Stella, holding me in her arms. *There was another picture I hadn't known about?* I couldn't have been more than a day or two old, my tiny wings spread out behind me as I laid my head on Stella's shoulder. Stella wore the same wistful expression she had in the more recent picture. Like she knew what she held in her arms was no longer hers. Tears ran down my face.

"It's yours to keep, sweetie. I wasn't sure when to tell you all this, but Stella told me to give you this picture when the time was right."

I hugged her. "You're the best. I'm glad you were such good friends with her—I'd love to know more about her."

She took a deep breath and perched on the arm of my chair, taking my hand in hers. "She was beautiful, kind, generous, and a wonderful friend. By the time she confided in me that she was a faerie, I must have known on some level, because I wasn't too surprised. Though I was surprised when a few months later she told me that she was pregnant. I hadn't ever met her husband, but he didn't seem to be the most upstanding sort. He left her when she was only a few months away from her due date."

My mouth fell open. "You . . . you don't know about my dad?"

"What do you mean?" Mom asked, genuine confusion on her face.

"Corrine met Stella about two years ago. Stella told her that my dad, who was also a Pure One, disappeared under weird circumstances and—"

"*Also* a Pure One? Are you saying that Stella was a Pure

One? I never knew." Mom's voice was little more than a whisper. She turned very pale. "Wait a second. Wouldn't that mean that you're . . ."

I nodded. "Yeah."

"But . . . but they don't exist here. They either left or were killed."

I gave her a look. "I'm standing right here."

This time it was her turn to sink into a chair. "I can't believe this. All this time . . . it explains why your wings look so different from everyone else's, so much brighter."

I put an arm around her shoulder. "Mom, Stella knew someone was after her. She wanted to protect me, but also you. By telling you she had a no-good husband run off on her, she probably thought she did you a favor."

Mom's face turned even paler. "She told me someone was after her, but I thought it was just because someone found out she was an unregistered faerie. It explains why she was so insistent that she couldn't raise you herself, why someone would have been after her."

"Someone who knew that Stella and my father were Pure Ones," I added.

Mom knitted her brows together. "So, if a Pure One mated with a half-faerie, what would that make the baby?"

"Still a half-faerie. There's this ancient faerie book— long story—it says that the offspring of anything other than two Pure Ones will simply have wings. They can fly but have no magic."

Mom coughed. "Don't take this the wrong way, Lila. I believe you about being Pure, but I've raised you since infancy, and I've never seen any signs of magic."

I sighed and sat back down again. "I'm sure. I just can't figure out the magic part. I didn't have time to finish reading the book. I'd give anything for another hour in that library."

Mom looked thoughtful. "You know, your wings have always been bright, but I've never seen them glow like they have this last week. Even tonight, they're brighter than they were before you went out of town."

"Yeah, I've been blinding people with their brilliance," I remarked sarcastically. "I wish I knew what it meant. It would be a downer if my only magic involves being the equivalent of a supercharged night-light."

"I'm sure it's more than that—your wings must be aware of the magic within you." Mom studied my face. "Maybe the magic only awoke recently, like a developmental thing." She swallowed hard. "And Lila—I'm so sorry I had to hide so much from you for so long. I hope you know it's because since the day Stella put you in my arms, I've felt like you were my own flesh and blood."

I hugged her. "I know. You're the best mom I could have asked for."

"I also hope you know how much Stella loved you. It tore her heart out the day she handed you over. She sacrificed everything to keep you safe."

"I know that, too. I just wish I knew if she's still alive. I don't think she could have returned to her own realm—she kind of stole a pretty important book." Imagine that: Stella didn't fit in with her own kind. Like mother, like daughter.

"Don't count her out, Lila. Stella told me that if the day were ever safe for faeries to live freely among people, she would return. I promised her I'd never move away from here unless I was forced to for your safety."

I stretched my arms overhead, yawning. "I'd love to believe she's out there somewhere."

"You better get some sleep, sweetheart. You've had a long week, and this one could be even longer." She kissed me on the cheek.

"Yeah, I'm just going to call Ash and make sure he's okay." My heart sank when I dialed his number and heard the despondence in his voice. Still no word from Corrine. All he got when he dialed her number was her voice mail. He'd left her seven messages and hadn't heard a thing.

"I'm sorry," was all I could offer him.

"Yeah. See you tomorrow," Ash said, and hung up.

I knew I was the sole reason he was even going to school tomorrow. If he didn't feel responsible for me, he would have his mom call him in sick so he could stay home and wait for Corrine. How would he even pretend to focus on schoolwork knowing his sister was missing? It made my problems seem less important—at least I was still safe and secure, for the moment.

I placed the picture of Stella holding me on the nightstand next to my bed. Looking out the window, I saw the lights on at Mrs. Nesbaum's house. Something caught my eye in the darkness: a dark shape in front of her house. A car. I couldn't remember the last time a visitor was at her house, especially not this late. Maybe she had struck gold at one of the neighborhood bingo tournaments and found a nice widower to spend her time with. I smiled, thinking that my nosy neighbor might be less focused on everyone else if she had some happiness in her life.

Thoughts of Corrine filtered through my mind as I drifted to sleep. I wished I could do something to help. Although I'd only met her two days ago, the outspoken faerie had made a huge impression. Ash spoke of his sister with such reverence and awe; she clearly meant the world to him. I tossed and turned, a new worry assaulting me each time I approached the edge of sleep. As the minutes ticked past in a slow crawl toward morning, I resigned myself to a sleepless night.

. . .

I WAS SURROUNDED by thick woods, and stars twinkled overhead. A full moon lit up the ground through the trees. I inhaled the scent of cool air and gazed upward. Within seconds, a large black cloud zoomed across the sky, eclipsing the moon. The ground turned dark. I'd been certain that Ash had been near me a second ago, but all that surrounded me now was inky blackness. "Ash!" I yelled, stumbling over a tree root.

I fell against an old wooden door, splinters piercing my hand. It was the shack again. The door swung open. A swell of icy air came toward me from the depths of the ramshackle house. Around me, a chilling rain fell. Shivering, I tried to step away from the door but an unseen force pulled me inside. "Ash!" I screamed again, falling through the doorway into the house. The door slammed behind me. A dim light washed over the room. Strange laughter echoed as I frantically waited for my eyes to adjust to the surroundings. Corrine stood directly in front of me, mouthing a silent warning. She drifted closer and was less than a foot away when her mouth ceased its frantic alert, and her rose-colored wings began to tear apart. Corrine tumbled, bruised and bloody, at my feet . . .

I WOKE IN A COLD SWEAT, my heart a jackhammer in my chest. I wiped my face with the sheet and took a deep breath, but couldn't stop shaking. The dream could only mean one thing. Corrine was either in trouble or already dead.

34

UNQUIET

I was sure the dream meant the killer was close. I still felt I was being watched. All day, walking down the hall at school with Brooklyn or Ash, I'd feel a sudden alarm vibrate through me. It would come out of nowhere and last for a minute or two. I checked out everyone who passed by in the hallway, but no one appeared to be glaring at me or shadowing my moves.

The dream about Corrine was the only one I hadn't shared with Ash. He was miserable enough without hearing that I'd dreamed his sister was possibly dead. He still walked me to every class and sat with me at lunch, but he didn't eat, and the spark in his eyes had dimmed.

It was only Wednesday afternoon, and he had already stopped checking his cell phone every five minutes. Even Lexie, whose observational skills were limited to nail polish shades and the Hotness Quotient of each boy in school, asked Ash if he was okay in algebra class. "Ash, for someone with an HQ in the smokin' range, you look like someone killed your dog. I'll cheer you up if you let me." He ignored her.

I tried to talk to Ash at my locker. Even after opening it multiple times without finding anything horrific inside, I still cringed in anticipation each time I lifted the latch. Ash leaned back against the locker next to mine and watched while I grabbed my books.

I placed my hand on his cheek, wanting nothing more than to erase the look of despair on his face. "This is probably a dumb question, but has your mom tried calling the FPP? I mean, if they really are protecting faeries, maybe they can help."

Ash exhaled a long, slow breath as if he'd been holding it for hours. "Yeah, my mom talked to the guy in charge from the FBI; it was that Agent Heinrichsen from the news. He's looking into the case himself. He told my mom to call if she heard anything."

I bit my lip. "Did he say if they were any closer to catching the killer?"

"All he would say is they're working every possible lead." His fingers tightened their grip on his notebook.

I stroked his cheek. "Ash, what is it?"

He pulled away from my touch. "He said they're considering Corrine a likely fatality."

I gasped. "He said that?" My dream resurfaced and I pushed it away.

"Yeah, until she turns up somewhere, they're working under the assumption that she's a victim. He said that he couldn't give details but that there are other faeries who've disappeared in the last few days." He shrugged. "Must be why I've seen cops outside other schools this week."

The tears that Ash couldn't cry spilled down my own cheeks. "I wish there was something I could say to make things better."

He touched my hand and held it in his. "I know. The

only thing keeping me sane right now is the fact that you're okay. I couldn't bear losing you, too."

I wanted to say that they didn't know for sure that Corrine was lost, but I couldn't will the words from my mouth. Instead, I kissed Ash gently. "Want to come over for dinner?"

I knew he would refuse even as the words left my lips. He shook his head.

"Or I could come to your house if that's easier?"

Ash was silent a moment and looked down at the floor. "Look, I know you want to be there for me and I appreciate it. I need time to myself." He pulled his head up and looked at me like it pained him to do so. "Nothing has changed as far as my feelings for you, Lila. You have to know that, but my being around you doesn't help you the way other faeries do."

You help me in other ways, though. "It's no big deal."

Gabriel picked us up in Ash's truck and drove to my house. Ash didn't say a word during the ride.

Gabriel handed Ash his keys. "Take care, man. Call us if you hear news."

Ash barely brushed my lips with his before he left.

We entered the house, and Brooklyn's pacing routine went into full swing. Gabriel turned on a football game in the living room, saying he needed some mindless entertainment. Brooklyn followed me into the kitchen, alternating between discussing her concerns about Ash with her bad feelings about what had happened to Corrine. I decided it was time to ask her for help. Maybe giving Brooklyn something to do would distract her from her constant pacing. After an early dinner, Gabriel went back to the television, and I whispered to Brooklyn, who nodded. I complained loudly for Mom's benefit about the pile of homework waiting for me. I grabbed two diet sodas and motioned for Brooklyn to follow me.

We sat cross-legged on my quilted bedspread, my clothes strewn over a chair and my school papers covering the floor. Cleaning and organization were overrated. Being neat and organized hadn't given me the control I thought it would.

"So what's up?" Brooklyn asked.

"I've been sitting in school for two whole days trying to figure out my magic," I admitted. "And I still have no clue. I can't protect myself and you guys without it, but I have no idea where to start. My math skills seem to be failing here— I've analyzed everything to death, trying to make the equation fit, but I keep coming up with zilch."

I stretched, and my wings glittered in the dim light of my room.

"They're so pretty," Brooklyn said, gazing at them.

"Thanks. I wish they could talk and tell me how to use my magic. It's not like I can stop a killer with pretty wings."

"Good point. So where do we start?" asked Brooklyn. "Are you psychic?"

I shook my head. "No, but I have some dreams that seem . . . different from regular ones."

Brooklyn looked thoughtful. "I'm writing that down, in case it's important. Dreams." She jotted the word down on a notepad. "Okay, next. What about mind control? Go ahead; try to make me do something."

I surveyed my untidy room. Two weeks ago, I would've had a heart attack just looking at this mess. "Clean up my room," I said.

"Not a chance," said Brooklyn. "We'll cross that one off."

We sat in silence for a few minutes. Brooklyn's eyes brightened and she jumped off the bed. "Wait! Try to make

Ash do something. Your wings only glow when he touches you. Maybe your magic has to do with him."

I made a wish with all my heart. "I want Ash to call me this instant."

We stared at the phone next to my bed. A full minute passed, but it remained silent. Nothing.

"Ring, damn it," I said in frustration. The second the words left my mouth, the phone rang. Brooklyn jumped, and I grabbed the phone.

"Hello . . . Ash?" I asked in a breathless voice. Silence. "Hello? Anyone there?"

I set the phone back down on the table. "That's strange. There was no one there."

Brooklyn frowned. "What did the Caller ID show?"

"Nothing—it's blank. Weird."

"What's also weird is that your wings were just glowing." She scribbled like mad on the notepad.

I twisted around to survey my wings. I spent a few more minutes willing Ash to call to no avail.

"This is stupid," I said at last. "If Ash has anything to do with my magic, I sure as heck don't understand what it is. How magic am I? I can't even get my own boyfriend to call me."

"Lila, he's going through a lot right now, but it's obvious how much he loves you." Brooklyn tried to sound reassuring. "As far as the magic thing, I feel like we're close—like it's right in front of us if we only knew where to look. Try again."

"Fine. Ash Cooper will call me on the phone . . . now! NOW!"

The stillness stretched from seconds into minutes. Nothing. I tried over and over asking, demanding, and finally pleading for Ash to call. The phone didn't ring.

After an hour, I groaned with exasperation. "I'm tired of this. Can we try again tomorrow?"

Brooklyn leaned back on the bed. "Sure. Don't worry, Lila. We'll figure this out. And I'm sure he'll call."

"Thanks, Brooklyn—for everything."

She smiled. "No worries. That's what faerie friends are for."

I lay there trying to piece together the puzzle but kept coming up short. What did glowing wings and a ringing phone have in common? This was not one of the logic questions on the standardized tests I took each year. Every once in a while I'd try again and wish that Ash would call right then. The phone stayed silent, as if punishing me for my selfish demands. Even as I drifted off to sleep, I couldn't sense an ounce of magic within me.

And Ash never called.

35

BELLS

All that filled my head the next morning was Ash's broken promise. He'd said he would call, and he didn't. Sure, there might've been a great reason—maybe news about Corrine that was so horrible he didn't want to talk about it. But if you really loved someone, you called them anyway. At least that was true for me—there was nothing so bad that I wouldn't have called him.

Unless he couldn't *call*, said a nagging voice in my head. I shook the thought from my mind and went downstairs to face a new day. Brooklyn sat at the table scanning the news on my laptop while eating a banana. Gabriel scooped cereal into his mouth at a rapid rate. Did all male faeries eat as much as he did?

"Anything new?" I asked.

"No, but I guess no news is good news," said Brooklyn. "I'd ask how Ash is, but I never heard the phone ring."

"Yeah, he never called, so your guess is as good as mine," I said, pouring some orange juice.

Brooklyn raised an eyebrow. "I'm sure he's fine."

Gabriel swallowed and looked up. "Yeah, the dude would have called if there was a problem."

"Right, which means he chose not to talk to me," I said.

Brooklyn frowned. "Okay, let's try to gain some perspective here. If he'd gotten bad news, we would have heard from him. What seems more likely is that he's depressed. He hasn't been the same this week, which has nothing to do with you and everything to do with Corrine."

I sighed. "I guess. I'm kinda new to this whole boyfriend thing."

"I get it." Brooklyn walked over to me and leaned on the counter. "I've had a few boyfriends myself. But unlike you, I've never had someone intent on dismembering me while I tried to enjoy a new relationship. I don't know how you're holding it together so well, Lila."

"I'm not." I gulped the rest of the juice and slammed the cup on the counter. A few orange droplets splattered onto the countertop. "Let's get to school. I want to see him, at least, so I know he's okay." I gestured to Gabriel. "Come on, we'll take Mom's car and you can drop us off. After school, we can work on my magic, which seems to be the ability to make guys disappear."

Gabriel smirked. "Buttercup, has anyone ever told you that you're too hard on yourself?"

"Must be another one of my 'gifts'," I said, grabbing my backpack.

Mom came in the room and I sensed another warning speech, so I kissed her and waved her off. "Gotta go, Mom. Call you later."

～

ASH WAS NOWHERE in sight when I reached my locker. I

sighed and grabbed my book for first period when I sensed someone behind me. The hairs on the back of my neck rose up.

"Where's loverboy? Did he leave you all alone?" A low voice growled in my ear.

I managed to turn my head and glare at Glen. "Get away from me."

He smirked. "I'd love to, but are you sure you want that?" His hand touched my ass. *Is he actually trying to feel me up in the middle of the hall?*

"Get your hand off me, creep." I tried to turn around but not before he pinched my butt hard.

"You gonna make me? All this time you act like a stuck-up bitch who's better than us, but you sure seem to be giving your boy some ass. Maybe I wanna see what I'm missing."

I spun around and kneed him hard in the groin. He crumpled to the ground, moaning. I leaned down and spoke slowly. "You wanna know what you're missing? What you'll be missing is a certain body part if you ever touch me again." I stormed off to class, leaving him clutching his junk on the floor while kids chuckled nearby.

Ash was waiting outside of first period class. I opened my mouth to speak, but before I could say anything, he grabbed me and pulled me to him. He kissed me once, softly, gently.

"I was so worried when you didn't call last night," I said. "No, that's not totally true. I was hurt, too. Sorry, I know that sounds selfish."

Ash caressed my cheek with his thumb. "No, I'm sorry. I've been really depressed, like, can't even get out of bed depressed. I don't know what's happened to her. What I do know is that whatever has happened, whatever will happen, I want you by my side."

Anger suddenly distorted his features. "I'm trying not to let this douchebag bring me down, you know?"

Unable to imagine his pain, I didn't say anything. Then, I leaned in and whispered in his ear, "I will do everything I can to end all this. I promise you that."

"I know," he said. "We better get in class."

In algebra, I tried to concentrate as Ms. Gable scribbled another formula on the board. The usually soothing precision of math annoyed me today. How could there be only one correct answer? It was unrealistic. The real world rarely offered such definitive solutions. If the whole serial killer problem had been like an algebraic equation, I could have solved it a long time ago.

And what was going on with Ash? I was relieved that he no longer seemed so despondent, but his change of personality was alarming. His reaction when he thought I'd rejected him proved that he could be impulsive when he was angry. What if his distress over his sister made him really unpredictable? *Please don't let him do anything stupid.* The drone of Ms. Gable's voice barely registered on my radar. Would this class never end? *Please let the bell ring and end my misery.* The bell rang.

"Good gravy," said Ms. Gable as the class filed out, "that's the second time this week the bell has rung early—I'm having a talk with the principal this instant."

"Wouldn't you rather talk to Mr. Turner?" a voice yelled on the way out the door. Ms. Gable's enraged expression did nothing to quell the laughter.

I walked with Ash and Brooklyn back to my locker. Halfway there, I stopped dead in my tracks.

"What is it?" asked Brooklyn, a look of alarm on her face.

"The bell rang early again."

Ash shrugged. "So? I'm not going to complain about it if it keeps getting us out of class."

"So . . . *I* wished the bell would ring, and it did. Just like with the phone last night," I said. "That's why there was no one on the line when it rang."

"Um, Lila, are you saying that you think your power is making bells ring?" asked Brooklyn, a dubious expression on her face.

Defensiveness rose in me. "I realize it's only a small step up from being a ginormous firefly, but it's all I can come up with."

"Then do it again," said Ash.

I wished for the bell to ring again. Nothing happened.

"Are you wishing?" asked Brooklyn.

"Yes," I said, my brows knit together. "Nothing."

"What exactly were you thinking about in class when you wished it to ring?" Ash asked.

"Well, I was upset, and I wanted out of there." We walked closer to my locker with our heads bent together.

"Maybe you need some emotion for it to work. Put some feeling into it when you do it this time," said Brooklyn.

This time, I imagined that I couldn't speak to Ash until the bell rang. The bell rang.

I glanced at my watch. "Oh, no big deal, it was supposed to ring then. It's the start of next period."

"So do it again," Ash urged.

I stared at him thinking of how much I loved him. I willed the bell to ring again. It did.

"What the hell is wrong with the bell?" asked a guy in a football jersey as he walked by.

"Dude, you're one rhyming mo-fo," his friend responded. Laughing, they turned the corner.

Brooklyn clasped my arm and jumped up and down. "You did it, Lila!"

"I think we should dial down the excitement level here," Ash said.

The hurt feelings returned. "But I figured out my magic."

Ash frowned at me.

"What?" I asked. "Oh, I get it. You think it's dumb. You were expecting I could turn invisible or bend time, but all I can do is ring bells. Is that it?"

Ash shook his head. "No Lila. I don't think it's dumb. I think maybe that's not all you can do, though, but it's a great start."

I turned to Brooklyn, who simply shrugged as if she agreed with him.

I was beyond irritated by the time we got to Birchester's chemistry class. They might not be overly impressed by my bell-ringing ability, but I'd show them. One minute into class, the bell rang. A minute later, it rang again. Then again. Mr. Birchester grumbled and called administration. He did not appear happy with the answer he got. The bell ringing increased in frequency, going off every ten to fifteen seconds. After a few more minutes of near constant ringing, he dismissed us in frustration, directing us to the cafeteria until the matter could be resolved. I smiled as the class exited around me, and raised an eyebrow at Ash and Brooklyn, who stared at me with open mouths. Good. Maybe now they'd appreciate my skills. I was a damn good bell ringer.

WHILE WE WERE EATING pizza in my room that evening, Brooklyn briefed Gabriel on my newfound "powers," then discussed the party we'd miss the following night.

"It's a shame we can't take Ash to that party tomorrow," Brooklyn said. "He needs a distraction."

I sighed. "I want to go myself, but Ash is right. It's too risky. Anyway, my mom would have a coronary before she'd let me go to a party."

Gabriel leaned back against a pillow, swallowing a huge bite of pepperoni pizza. "This is totally off topic, but I just wanted to say that this bed is way more comfy than the couch. You sure you girls wouldn't want a little company tonight?"

Brooklyn rolled her eyes at him, but I couldn't help laughing. There was so little to laugh about these days. I shifted on the bed. "Thanks, Gabriel but I think we'll manage." I tossed him another slice of pizza. "What are doing while we're in school all day, anyway?"

Gabriel answered while chewing. "Looking for signs of Corrine, scouring the woods—when I'm not staking out your school, that is."

Knowing he was watching out for us made me feel safer. "Thanks, Gabriel." I turned to Brooklyn. "I wanted to say sorry for chem class today. I was mad. I wanted to prove I wasn't worthless."

"No one thinks you're worthless, Lila." Brooklyn giggled. "That was an impressive show, though—did you see the look on Birchester's face when the bell kept ringing?"

"Yeah, I guess I went a little overboard."

Gabriel chuckled. "Wish I could have seen it. Ash is right, though. There's gotta be more to your magic than bells. I'd bet my wings on it."

I forced myself to exhale. "I hope you're right. It's hard to believe the fate of our kind would rest on a ringing bell. Let's hope I figure it out in time to be useful."

I willed Ash to call right then, but the phone remained

silent. Of course. I tried again. Wishing it would ring with all my might *and* thinking of how much I wanted to talk to Ash, the phone rang. But my desired caller was not on the other end. The line was dead.

Brooklyn and Gabriel sat with me late into the night. We discussed all the types of bells in the world and I practiced on the ones in the near vicinity. I made my alarm clock ring, my cell phone, and even the smoke alarm, which brought Mom running into the room.

Frustrated, I told Gabriel we could call it a night, and he followed Mom out of the room. He deserved to watch some ESPN after putting up with my lame magic. Rather than feeling empowered, I felt like a cheap party trick. Too bad Jacinda's party was a no-go—I could entertain everyone as Lila, the Mystical, Glowing, Bell-Ringing Faerie.

Brooklyn must've read my mind again. "Stop thinking sarcastic thoughts, Lila. I can see it in your face. Try sleeping on it and see if any ideas come to you in the morning."

The phone rang.

"Lila, stop it. It's late and you'll wake your mom."

"I didn't do it," I said, diving for the phone.

"Hello," I whispered into the receiver. "Ash? What's wrong?"

Brooklyn's eyes were wide.

"Oh my God," I repeated over and over again. "I'm so sorry, Ash . . . stay there . . . no, don't touch the gun . . . please . . . yes, I promise!" I hit the End button on the phone and sat very still, sobbing.

"What is it?" Brooklyn's voice screeched. "I'm going crazy here."

I blinked through my tears. I'd forgotten she was even in the room. I forced myself to focus on my friend, who was gripping the bedspread with white knuckles. "Ash is talking about using a gun. I can't calm him down. He got a text message tonight—it was from Corrine's phone but it wasn't from Corrine."

Brooklyn took a deep breath. "How do you know? What did it say?"

I tried to steady the shaking in my hands as I answered. "It said, 'Your faerie-bitch girlfriend is next.'"

36

JACKPOT

Thick clouds mask the moon, creating a blanket of darkness. I could not have asked for more perfect weather. I have much work to do regarding the One, but there is time and this opportunity is too good to pass up. Plus, it gives me an opportunity to get rid of some evidence.

I pull the bloody cell phone from my pocket. Burying it, I realize that after I take down the One, I will relish killing this particular she-bitch. I finger the scab on my face, grimacing.

The One's magic has almost reached its potential, all because of love. Such a wasteful emotion. Doesn't she realize how revolting she really is? No matter, she will soon be out of the way, and there will be no more like her on earth. tracking the rest of the half-ones will take some time, but it will be easy—like squashing mosquitoes.

I survey the building ahead of me, not believing my good fortune. The gods, wherever they are, are surely favoring me to bring so many mosquitoes. After this, I will find her—and end her. Then I will be able to end them all.

37

REACTION FORMATION

F riday morning, I was scared . . . and sick. Someone had hurt Corrine, or worse. Now they were trying to intimidate me. I didn't tell Mom about the text message. If she knew, I'd be in my room all day with police at the house, which wouldn't do much good. Nothing would stop the killer. It might even make it easier for him, since there would be fewer witnesses in my house than in a packed school. Not that I planned on staying at school. Sure, I'd go so that Mom didn't suspect anything. But then I was taking off to find Corrine, with or without help—although I hoped it'd be the former.

If only I'd woken up with answers. Instead, all I got was sickness. I'd vomited five times before five a.m., and still had nausea worse than ever before. Since getting out of bed, each step threatened to send me over the edge. Waves of illness rocked me every few minutes.

"I know you must be terrified, but we're here for you, Lila," Brooklyn said as she applied my bindings. My wings didn't even protest; they felt ill too.

"I know. I just want to be there for you guys too," I said, trying not to gag as my stomach roiled again.

"You will be. The answers will find you, Lila. I know they will."

"It would be nice if it happened sooner rather than later."

We went downstairs for breakfast, although there was no way I could keep anything down. Nothing would betray my condition to Mom faster than vomiting all over the kitchen. Brooklyn and I passed by Gabriel, who remained asleep on the couch, until the sound of Brooklyn opening the refrigerator door prompted an abrupt awakening.

"I need food," he said, rubbing the sleep from his eyes as he stumbled in to join us. He poured a bowl of cereal, and I wanted to tell him about the crazy message but didn't want any chance of Mom overhearing us. I'd wait until we were on the way to school.

I glanced at my cell. "Gabriel, can you hurry it up? Ash is waiting for us at school." He couldn't know how much everything had changed for me since bedtime.

Gabriel raised an eyebrow at me, then took another spoonful, talking and crunching at the same time. "Don't you know that breakfast is the most important meal of the day?"

I sighed and was reaching for a banana to stow in my backpack when Mom rushed into the kitchen. Her mouth was set in a tight line, her face as white as the Formica countertop. She gripped the edge like it was the only thing keeping her upright.

"Lila," she said in a controlled voice, "you're not going to school today."

"Why?" I asked, feigning innocence. How on earth could she know about the text message unless Ash told her?

"It's all over the morning news," Mom said, starting to shake.

Now I was frightened. "What was on the news? Mom?"

Mom gulped. "Apparently there was an FPP shelter in Raleigh."

"Was?" Brooklyn and I asked in unison. Gabriel stopped eating.

"It happened sometime last night, while they were sleeping. This morning they found the remains of twenty-two faeries and two staff members."

The words sliced me like knives, and I barely made it to the sink before I threw up again.

Gabriel punched the countertop with his fist.

"Oh.My.God," said Brooklyn. "How?"

"It sounded like some sort of gas was used. After they were unconscious, he removed their wings. How could he have known where the shelter was?" Mom asked, sounding on the verge of hysteria.

"I don't know, Mom," I said as a sense of dread came over me. How *did* he seem to find faeries so easily? He'd managed to take out an entire shelter at once, and make me weaker. So he could kill me next.

Weaker. I was definitely weaker today; that was why I felt so ill. I hadn't been sick until the murders started. Individual killings made me puke; a whole shelter of faeries in one fell swoop made me feel like death.

Brooklyn looked concerned and reached out to take my arm. Her fingers felt cold but comforting. "Are you okay, Lila? You look funny."

"I'm not sure." In truth, I felt better the second Brooklyn touched me.

Several seconds later, the nausea dissipated further

when Gabriel laid his hand on my shoulder. "Buttercup, we've got your back. This guy can't get through me."

"Ms. Kincade," said Gabriel, "Even though Brooklyn will be with Lila all day, I'm going to stay close to the school in case there's trouble."

Mom shook her head. "I don't think it's the best idea to go to school today."

It broke my heart to see the grief on Mom's face. "Look, I'd be safer in a crowded school than here. At least I have more of a chance if I'm surrounded by a ton of people. If I feel strange at all, I'll have Gabriel and Brooklyn bring me here." *After I find Corrine.*

"I don't like it." Mom groaned.

"I won't leave her side, Ms. Kincade," said Brooklyn. "I promise."

"Mom," I said quietly, "I don't think you should stay here either. He knows where I live. Can you go to one of your friends' for the day? Or work extra hours at the office?"

Mom shook her head as she followed me outside. "I'm staying right here, Lila." A heavy mist surrounded us, and we could barely see the trees through the fog.

"Is that you, Lila?" a thin voice called.

I turned and spotted a figure veiled in the vapor.

"Who is that?" asked Gabriel. His hand reached into his waistband, and I realized he must have a weapon on him. He stepped in front of me, forming a protective barrier between the figure and me.

"Just me, dear. It's Nelly." The elderly woman emerged from the trees separating her yard from mine.

"Hi, Mrs. Nesbaum. We're on our way to school," I said, baffled at the appearance of my neighbor. She tended to be a late-afternoon to early evening snooper—morning snooping was a first for her.

"It's good to see you with friends, Lila," Mrs. Nesbaum said. "Why don't you come over for tea one day this weekend?"

"Sure, sounds good. Well, I better get going." I stopped. "Wait, can my mom hang out with you today? She needs some, um, advice."

Mrs. Nesbaum smiled at Mom. "Come on over, dear, I've got the teakettle going."

"I'm not sure about this," Mom said, but I knew she didn't want to say too much in front of our neighbor.

"Nonsense," said Mrs. Nesbaum. "Let the children go to school. Come with me."

Mom hugged me tight, then reluctantly receded into the mist with our neighbor.

"Weird," I said as I climbed into the passenger seat next to Gabriel. "I've lived next to her for sixteen years, and she's never invited us over before."

"She seems nice enough," said Brooklyn. "Definitely not a serial killer."

Gabriel navigated the fog on the windy road to school, while I stared out the window. Brooklyn filled him in on the text message Ash had gotten from Corrine's phone. "I can't even imagine what he must be going through." She sniffled from the back seat. "Poor Corrine."

I touched Gabriel's arm. "I'm worried about him, Gabriel. I'm afraid he's going to get himself hurt."

His eyes remained straight ahead. The road wasn't visible save for a few feet in front of the car. After a minute, he spoke. "He was probably trying to hold on to some shred of hope about Corrine, but the text message shattered that all to hell. If something happened to you, Lila . . . I don't know what he'd do."

"If only the police could do their job and catch the killer," said Brooklyn.

Gabriel's fingers clutched the steering wheel. "Trust me, if Ash doesn't kill that psycho, I will."

Staring at Gabriel's muscular body, I thought he might not even need a weapon to do the job. *But the killer took out an entire shelter of faeries.* Even though he'd used gas, surely someone had woken up and tried to fight.

We rode in silence for several minutes, the tension in the car as thick as the humid air. Though still a train wreck, having two faeries in such close proximity had really helped my physical condition. The sickness was all but gone. If only Gabriel could come to school with me too. I glanced at Gabriel and Brooklyn. "Hey, can you guys feel when other faeries are around?"

Brooklyn tilted her head as if thinking, but Gabriel shook his head immediately.

"No, I've tried before. When I was living at the house with Corrine, I'd hear the front door open and try to sense whether it was a human or a faerie. I got it right about fifty percent of the time, go figure," said Gabriel.

"I've never noticed any feelings like that," said Brooklyn. "Why? Can you?"

"Yeah, but I think it only started recently," I said.

"Around the same time as your magic ring-a-ding-ding ability?" asked Gabriel.

"I guess so." I almost mentioned the sickness part too, but didn't want them to worry that a faerie was dying every time I felt a little queasy. What good would it do to share my misery? Something also stopped me from mentioning my plan about finding Corrine—maybe because it looked like only her body would be found at this point.

As we pulled into school, I spotted Ash's truck. It was

empty. Gabriel grabbed my arm before I could get out. Yeah, he was strong. "Listen up, buttercup. Anything funny happens, call my cell. Anyone even looks at you strange, call. I won't be far from the school." He turned his gaze toward Brooklyn. "Don't leave her side. At least Ash is here —the more people around Lila the better."

I studied him as I climbed out of the car. "But you're a faerie too. Are you sure it's safe to be driving around by yourself?"

"No worries," said Gabriel, lifting his shirt to reveal the butt of a handgun. He threw up a peace sign as he drove away.

I waved. Every good-bye was somehow more meaningful now, like it might be the last. My feet didn't seem to want to obey as I trudged into school, and poor Brooklyn had to endure the death grip I had on her arm.

"Sorry," I said, loosening my hand.

Brooklyn gave me a reassuring squeeze. "It's okay, Lila. We won't be more than inches from you all day."

Ash wasn't at my locker. Frowning, I waited until the final bell rang before dashing to algebra with Brooklyn. Ash was in his usual seat at the back of the room. He looked up, noticeable black circles underneath his eyes. His gaze briefly met mine before Ms. Gable began class. Reluctantly, I took my seat. I turned around and noticed Ash had put his head down on his desk. He must not have slept at all last night.

"Who wants to take us through the first problem?" Ms. Gable asked.

It was my first time going to class without my homework. Doing math in the face of dying seemed ludicrous. Ms. Gable was surprisingly easy on me, and suggested I get more rest over the weekend. *I'll have enough time to rest when I'm dead.*

As class continued, Ms. Gable's voice receded into the background. I closed my eyes, drifting away in my mind. I felt Brooklyn's faerie-ness, a warm source of energy protecting me. Smiling, I basked in the acute sensory perception and tried to sense other faerie energy in the room. *There is another.* My eyes flew open. I glanced around the room, trying to appear nonchalant. I surveyed the attire of the kids, but the boys all wore loose T-shirts like Gabriel, and there were more fashion-challenged girls than I'd realized.

As people exited class, I couldn't believe how many hoodies and T-shirts I saw—except for Lexie, of course. She was sporting another skin-tight shirt with lettering across her chest that might as well have spelled *I need attention.*

When I told Brooklyn about the other faerie, she said she couldn't feel the faerie energy. Excitement wasn't even the word for what I felt. There were others like me in the school, and they were in Hiding too. I vowed to find out who they were if I survived the week.

I stopped at Ash's desk. His head was still down, and he snored lightly.

"Ash?" I gently placed my hand on top of his head.

Ash jumped up from the chair, disoriented. "Corrine? What's going on?" His eyes cleared and focused on me. "Oh, hi."

Brooklyn and I steered him out of the room as Ms. Gable watched. "It seems you *all* need to get a little more sleep," she called after us.

"I've been worried sick about you," I said once we were in the hallway.

"Yeah," said Ash, but his eyes were empty.

"Ash? Can you look at me please?" I put my hand under his chin and turned his face toward mine. "You're scaring me."

That snapped him out of his trance. "You have nothing to be scared of, Lila. I'm not going to let anything happen to you." He patted his shirt, the unmistakable outline of a gun underneath.

Brooklyn gasped, looking up and down the hallway. "Ash! You can't have a gun in school. Do you know what will happen if you get caught?"

Ash shrugged and I grabbed his arm. "She's right. How will you be able to protect me if you're behind bars?"

He didn't say anything. He seemed a million miles away. Fear gripped me. There was no way I was telling him about my plan to find Corrine.

This time I shook him. "Seriously, Ash—where did you get that? Did Gabriel find a two-for-one deal?"

Ash laughed bitterly. "No, he's always had a gun—because he's Gabriel. But when I asked him for one, he wouldn't give it to me. So I went out last night and got my own. No offense, but this has a little more stopping power than bell ringing."

The comment stung, but he was right. I kept hold of his arm, but Ash stiffened. "I don't mean to scare you, Lila. But for me, there's no choice. No one is taking you away from me." He shrugged. "It's all up to us. That Heinrichsen guy called this morning. They're trying to track Corrine's phone using GPS crap, but it won't matter. He also suggested that I not respond to any more messages from psychopaths."

As I opened my mouth, Jacinda sauntered up to us and gave a knowing smile when she saw my hand on Ash. "So guys, you comin' tonight or what?" she asked. "It's gonna be chill—my cousin got a keg."

"It's looking doubtful," Brooklyn said quickly. "Lila got herself in some trouble and she's sort of grounded the whole weekend."

Jacinda looked me up and down. "You, grounded? Damn, girl. I didn't figure you for a troublemaker. Well, the rest of you are invited too, so see if you can get your girl here out of parent jail." She ran down the hall toward Jake.

Brooklyn nudged me toward chem class. "We better get in there."

Ash kissed my hand before we went into the lab. "Don't worry about me. It's you we need to worry about."

I let my hand drop as we entered the room.

The bell rang, on its own. I wasn't in the mood for tricks today. Dylan started chatting up Brooklyn as soon as she sat down. I felt Ash's tired eyes burning into me, keeping watch.

Mr. Birchester lectured about their next experiment. Next to me, Jacinda doodled hearts and a list of snack options for the party, her long, lacquered nails clicking against the pen. Jacinda hummed softly to herself as she wrote. *It must be nice to live in a world where you can plan parties and dance the night away with your boyfriend.* I sensed around the room and realized that aside from Brooklyn, there were no faeries in this class.

No faeries. Corrine popped into my head again. *Find Corrine.* What was that about? The chances of her being alive were slim to none. Still. I glanced around the room. Brooklyn remained engrossed in her quiet conversation with Dylan. Ash was facedown by his beaker, sound asleep. Maybe no one would notice. I whispered to Jacinda that I was going to the bathroom and slipped out the door.

I'd only gotten a short distance down the hall when the pain hit. Pain that packed such intensity, I clutched my stomach in agony. Retching, I tried to recall the location of the nearest restroom. Down the hall, around the corner. If only I could make it that far before puking. Footsteps ran in the opposite direction, but when I turned the corner, there was no one there. At least I wasn't the only one running this time. *Please, please, let me make it to the bathroom.* I threw myself into the door and pushed it open.

Holy mother of God. A girl lay face down on the floor, a pool of blood spreading beneath her. Her back had two thin lines of blood where wings had been, but the gushing blood was coming from the severed seracord. The girl whimpered. I rushed to her and knelt down on the cold tile, then turned, vomiting on the floor. I grasped the dying girl's hand, knowing that nothing could be done.

"It's okay," I lied, smoothing the girl's hair with her free hand in a desperate attempt to comfort her. I ignored the continued churning in my gut. Moving the girl's hair, I saw her face. Carrie Ann Pruitt, a quiet girl who was in several classes with me.

"It . . . was . . ." Carrie Ann tried to speak. With the amount of blood pouring out of her, she didn't have much time left.

I continued smoothing her tangled, blood-soaked hair. "I know. I know. Do you know who did this to you?"

Carrie Ann opened her mouth. "Yes," she said weakly. Her lips moved again slowly, without sound, then stopped. Her hand slipped from mine.

"No," I whispered. Silent tears streamed down my face. I sat with her, senselessly tucking a stray hair behind her ear. Realizing I was about to vomit again, I raced into a stall.

At that moment, the bathroom door opened and someone came in. I fought for control over my wayward stomach. A second passed, then came a girl's hysterical screams, and footsteps echoed through the hall. "Call 911! I think she's dead—there's so much blood!"

I didn't want to leave Carrie Ann, but being questioned by the police was not an option. I had no choice. I had to run.

GRAND PRIZE WINNER

Ding-ding-ding. *The winner has been determined, ladies and gentlemen. Or rather, the loser. Now that I know it's her, I realize I should have been more patient. My impatience has always been a bit of an issue—even as a child I was tempestuous at times. But that carrie ann practically begged me to kill her by going alone to the bathroom. Crimes of opportunity don't come around every day, though I admit that I lost control once I followed her inside. But once again, luck must be on my side, because if I hadn't killed her, I wouldn't have discovered the One.*

Lila.

CHAOS THEORY

Mass chaos ensued as teachers tried but failed to contain students in the classrooms. Students who heard the screaming from the hall must have texted all their friends; a stampede of footsteps and loud voices went by the bathroom. My heart raced. I could slip in with the crowd and maybe the blood wouldn't be as noticeable.

"LILA!"

Ash's voice could be heard above all others. *Oh no!* He'd heard the girl screaming and thought I was the dead one.

"Ash! I'm here!" Scanning the crowd, I spotted Ash and Brooklyn in the midst of everyone.

Ash sprinted toward me, not stopping until his arms locked around mine. "Oh, thank God! Where did you go?" He looked me over. "You're bleeding! What the hell is going on?"

"It's not my blood. We have to go."

Brooklyn caught up to us, and Ash whispered, "Let's move." His hand remained at his hip, as if he was going to whip out his gun and order everyone to stay back.

The overhead announcement system crackled. "This is Mr. Turner. Everyone, please remain calm. The police are now on the premises and have requested that everyone remain where they are."

Right. Too late. This was clearly not part of the school's emergency evacuation plan. I swept along on a tide of students. My legs felt like rubber, and I struggled to regain my footing.

"Hold on to my arm and don't let go," Ash instructed me.

I sensed the presence of another faerie near me, but there were kids everywhere, and the feeling was lost a minute later. The exit was less than fifty feet away when there was a surge in the crowd behind us. Pressure from the swell of students threw us toward the lockers lining the side of the hallway, and my back scraped against the last locker on the right side.

I felt the binding rip on my right wing. Instinctively, I reached to check the wing and let go of Ash's arm for a second. I watched in horror as he and Brooklyn were swept away from me.

"Lila!" he screamed. "Head for the door and stay put once you get outside—"

I couldn't hear anymore over all the other shouts in the hallway, and in a minute, Ash disappeared from view. Bodies pressed in on me from every side and I fought to reach the exit. Another surge came from behind and pushed me out the door into the parking lot.

Ash stood about twenty feet away, frantically scanning the crowd and calling my name. I ran over and wrapped my arms around him. We stood with Brooklyn, surveying all the students huddled in frightened groups. Jacinda was nearby, telling everyone to still come over that night—that they could support each other and remember their classmate. I attempted to hide behind Ash, hoping the blood wasn't too noticeable.

The police blocked the parking lot so no cars could enter or exit. A Channel 9 news van was already parked along the side of the road, and Mr. Turner attempted to keep the female reporter from approaching the students.

I leaned over to catch my breath, and my binding ripped further. My right wing began to unfurl. *Crap.* This was so not good.

"My wing," was all I said under my breath to Ash, and took off running.

"Hey," yelled Brooklyn, "you can't leave us again. Where are you going?"

I didn't look back. I ran as fast as my legs would pump across the parking lot.

"Wait up," Ash called, his footsteps gaining ground behind me. I glanced over my shoulder—and tripped. An explosion of pain shot through my face as it connected with asphalt. Sprawled on the pavement, hands stinging, I knew the trickle dripping from my nose was blood. *At least now I have an excuse for my bloody shirt.*

"Lila, here, let me help you up." Mr. Finch stood above me, reaching his hand down to help. I grasped it, mumbling a thank you.

I wanted to warn him, but wanted to get out of there even more. "It's not safe for us here, Mr. Finch." There was no use pretending I didn't know.

He nodded. "I know, but you should be back with the other students—it's safer for you there," Mr. Finch said as Ash caught up to me. I felt my wing pressing against my shirt and knew the last shred of binding was about to give way.

Brooklyn caught up to us at that moment, huffing and

puffing. "Holy cow," she said, "I need a minute to catch my breath—"

"No time," said Ash. He grabbed my hand and we took off.

"Be careful, Mr. Finch," I managed to yell. He wasn't muscular like Gabriel, and didn't look like he could fight off Ms. Gable, let alone a killer.

"Wait," Mr. Finch yelled, but a reporter walked up to him, and while he was distracted, we raced across the street and into the trees.

We texted Gabriel to pick us up few blocks away to avoid the main campus and kept running.

Brooklyn gasped. "This would be so much easier if we could just fly."

"Yeah, I know." I looked over my shoulder. My shirt poked straight out on the right side where my wing was attempting to expand.

"How's your nose?" Ash asked.

I touched it as I ran. "It hurts like hell, but I don't think it's broken."

Ash's phone rang and he spoke in ragged breaths in between steps. "Got it, and tell my mom we're okay," he said before hanging up. He turned toward us. "Gabriel went to Rock Haven Road—he's waiting for us there."

I realized Mom would soon hear that a faerie was killed at Northeast. I pulled out my cell phone to let her know I wasn't dead. It rang before I could dial, and I promised her I was on my way. So much for finding Corrine.

Gabriel was on the side of the road. I dove into the back-seat to prevent anyone else from seeing my errant wing. Ash jumped in back with me and Brooklyn rode up front with Gabriel.

"Damn, I'm glad you guys are okay. This guy is off-his-rocker crazy doing that at school—he'll be caught for sure." Gabriel glanced at my shirt in the rearview mirror. "You sprung, huh?"

Ash worked on taping down my wing with the car kit, while Brooklyn scanned the road ahead. Figuring the whole of the Chapel Hill police force was occupied at Northeast, Gabriel floored the gas pedal. We careened into my driveway as Mom ran out to us from Mrs. Nesbaum's house.

We sprinted into the house and I dead-bolted the door. Mom's eyes were swollen from crying. "Oh, thank the Lord," she said, hugging me tight.

We raced to turn on the news. The persistent reporter had evidently gotten to several kids, as well as Mr. Finch, before Mr. Turner could intervene. They were giving dramatic details of the evacuation and third-hand accounts of the murder.

"This girl Tina said Mary Jo was the one who found her . . . and there was blood everywhere . . . even on the walls," one brunette gushed to the sympathetic-looking reporter.

Sitting in dismal silence, we watched the news for any new developments. I curled up next to Ash on the couch, while Mom sat on my other side. Gabriel and Brooklyn stationed themselves in opposite armchairs like guardian angels. I closed my eyes in the midst of the group, trying to discern more understanding of my magic. I came up blank. While I did get a strong sense of each faerie around me, that ability would soon be useless if all the faeries were dead. Time was definitely not on my side.

A picture of the deceased student went up on the television screen, and I really wished the sound were a little louder. This was a story I wanted to hear. The volume level on the television rose although the remote control lay untouched on the coffee table. No one else seemed to notice. So I could control more than bells, and I had to have strong emotions, but not necessarily connected to Ash.

"It has been confirmed that the victim of the murder today at Northeast High was Carrie Ann Pruitt. She was a junior, and is believed to be yet another victim of the killer police are now calling the Wing Collector."

"They've named him?" Gabriel asked in amazement. "Un-freakin'-believable."

"Yeah," said Ash. "I'm sure he's loving it. What's wrong with the media?"

I blinked away tears. Carrie Ann's life had run out onto a faded, green-tiled bathroom floor. No one should die like that. Though I hadn't suspected Carrie Ann was a faerie, it made sense. She'd been a loner, like me. I'd been so concerned with keeping my own profile low that I hadn't paid much attention to anyone else.

"Are you kidding me?" Ash turned the television off and threw the remote control at a pillow, snapping me back to the present.

I looked at him. "What?"

"They didn't get him . . . he got away. The guy was right there under their noses, and they couldn't find him," Ash said in disgust.

"It's up to us," I said. I sat up straighter on the couch and squared my shoulders.

"What do you mean?" asked Brooklyn.

"No one else is going to catch this guy. It's either going to be us finding him, or us getting killed. I feel it." I debated sharing my ability to influence the television, but decided that remote volume control wouldn't exactly inspire confidence. I also didn't share that thoughts of Corrine kept surfacing in my mind. Corrine was somehow still a part of things.

"Young lady, you're not going *anywhere* to catch *anyone*," Mom said. "You all are staying right here in this house. There has to be someone competent in the police department."

"Competence doesn't seem to be their main hiring criteria," said Ash.

Gabriel jerked his thumb at Ash. "What he said. They've totally supported the lame-ass mating law."

I listened to the exchange, staring at the woman who'd raised me with such love and protection. Now it was my turn to protect Mom by keeping my plan a secret. I wouldn't tell her that I was going out tonight. But I was going. I couldn't explain why I had to be there, but I knew it was important and that it was a party I couldn't miss. I also had a strange feeling it might be my only one.

Mom set up an air mattress for Ash on the floor, since Gabriel said he wasn't giving up the couch. Ash had told his mom he couldn't leave me and insisted he would stay in touch. It was going on ten o'clock and I urged Mom to turn off the news and go to bed.

"They aren't going to tell you anything good, Mom. Just get some sleep. Please."

A little past ten, Mom finally silenced the television and told me to wake her if anybody needed anything. After waiting several minutes, I texted Ash, telling him to bring Gabriel to my room. Brooklyn eyed me quizzically but didn't say anything. When they arrived, I told them my plan. "I'm going to Jacinda's."

"Have you completely lost your mind, buttercup?" asked Gabriel.

"Lila," Ash pleaded, "this is the least safe thing you could do right now."

"Oh please. Stop talking to me like I'm nuts." I met Ash's eyes. "Look, I don't want to go to Jacinda's to party. The killer is going to be there—I know it."

"What?" asked Ash, trying to keep his voice low. "You seem to know a lot of things lately."

I shrugged. "I think my senses have grown a lot in the last few days for some reason. If he finds me at home, I think he'll win. You can't guard me forever—we'll fall asleep at some point."

"This guard won't ever be down," said Gabriel, fingering the revolver beneath his shirt.

"I appreciate that," I said. My voice was calm, but I wanted to scream at the top of my lungs. *Being hunted is not something anyone can stop.* I steadied my nerves. "But I think the more we wait, the more the odds are in his favor. I want to end this before anyone else gets killed. I'm tired of waiting to see if each day will be the day he tries to kill me. So we go to the party and find him."

"Um, don't take this the wrong way, Lila," said Brooklyn, "but you sound like you're ready for him and, well . . . are you? Have you discovered your magic, beyond the bells, I mean?"

I cleared my throat. "Not entirely, but it's coming along."

Ash pulled me into the corner of the room and grasped my hands in his. "Lila, I want to do what's best here. You seem more confident than I've ever seen you, but I'm not sure what there is to be confident about. We could all die tonight."

I leaned forward and pressed my lips to his. I lingered there a minute, thinking of all the what-ifs that could have been if we'd had a little longer to date each other.

"I know that. I realize the likelihood of us growing old together, sitting in our rocking chairs drinking sweet tea and playing cribbage is slim. But this is the only real chance I think we have." I kissed him again. "And I know your mother lost a child already this week, so I totally understand if you want to stay with her. No mother should have to lose both her children."

Ash gritted his teeth, and his eyes were wet. "It happens all the time in war, Lila. And this is a war—just a different kind. I go where you go." He turned to Gabriel and Brooklyn with a shrug. "I guess it's settled then. I'm going too."

"Let's do it, then," said Gabriel. "I, for one, am so sick of this shit. 'The Wing Collector' my ass. This guy is goin' down. Tonight."

Gabriel and Brooklyn engaged in some quick planning for the evening. Ash cracked a half smile at me. "Cribbage? I had no idea. We'll have to wait a long time, because I don't know anyone under eighty years old who plays it."

I gave him a seductive look. "You completely underestimate cribbage."

Ash whispered in my ear, "Then I challenge you to a game of strip cribbage if we get through this in one piece. That's the only way I can see it being fun."

It was his first flirtatious comment since Corrine's disappearance, and I almost cried with relief at the glimmer of his old self. I arched my eyebrow to let him know I'd consider his suggestion.

The weight of the night ahead hit me, and I scribbled a note, pushing aside the thought that it could be my last communication with Mom. Just in case, I grabbed a photo of the two of us together from my scrapbook and placed it with the note: *I love you.* I was six in the picture, smiling up at her as she held a dripping ice-cream cone. A gentle nudge from Ash brought me out of the reverie.

I grabbed the mace and a small kitchen knife, which I asked Ash to carry. I didn't trust my ability to use it and didn't think it would be helpful if I accidentally impaled myself. With two guns and a knife between us, we were well armed. Yet we might as well be wielding plastic swords for all the good they'd do against this monster. We slipped out the bedroom window, dropping off the ledge and into the grass below. The night was clear and a full moon lit up the sky. I felt a sudden wave of déjà vu but shook it off.

I waited impatiently with Brooklyn while Gabriel and Ash got Ash's truck. Gabriel put it in neutral and pushed it down the drive before starting it so we wouldn't wake Mom.

We coasted along the winding road, the headlights slicing through the night. The air was downright chilly, a refreshing change from the damp stickiness that had lasted long past its time. An image of Corrine popped into my mind. I shook my head, but still saw Corrine and her pink highlights as clearly as if she were right there. Why was I seeing dead faeries?

"At least it will be a beautiful night to die," said Brooklyn, whose apparent knack for mind-reading kicked in as she looked up at the sky.

Gabriel grunted. "Yeah, but we're not the ones that are gonna be doing the dyin'."

We heard the music from blocks away. The thump of the bass permeated the air and I stared in amazement at the number of cars lining the street. *Half the student population of Northeast is at this party*. It certainly had more of a party vibe than the memorial Jacinda had alluded to earlier. If I died tonight, at least I could say I'd been to a party.

Brooklyn peered out the window. "I can't believe the police haven't been called."

"The cops are too busy not catching the killer to worry about a little party," said Gabriel, contempt in his voice.

"Gabriel, I think maybe you should consider a career in law enforcement. You'd show them a thing or two," I offered, getting a half smile in return.

The closest parking spot was a few blocks away. Dozens of classmates milled around on the porch and in the front yard, carrying large plastic cups filled with undoubtedly cheap beer. The house was brightly lit, loud laughter spilling from the windows. We entered the front door, winding our way through a group dancing to a loud, pulsing rhythm. Ash kept his hand on my back the whole time.

"No way, girl! You made it," shrieked Jacinda when she spotted us from across the room. "I thought you were grounded. Some crazy shit going on at school today, huh? Is it bad I'm glad it isn't just black people getting killed anymore?"

"Amen, sister," said a girl near Jacinda. "Gives us a little breathing room, though Lordy help the gay black faeries."

"I thought this was going to be a memorial," I said.

"You know what, girl? I thought about if I died, would I want people to be mopin' around being all sad or would I want them to party in my honor? I'd want a party. So this party is a celebration of life in honor of Carrie Ann." She grinned. "Hey, let me get y'all some drinks."

"I have an extra," said a voice near us. Dylan appeared out of nowhere and handed a drink to Brooklyn.

"Thanks," said Brooklyn, "but I'd rather have Diet Coke."

"Got it," said Dylan, "I'll be right back."

"Can you make that two?" I asked.

"What?" said Jacinda. "You bust out of your house when you're supposed to be grounded, and you're not gonna drink anything good?"

I smiled at Jacinda and watched the room. "Yeah, I'm lame that way. It sure is a big party."

"I do love to entertain," said Jacinda.

Beer spilled from the cups of enthusiastic dancers,

bright orange Cheetos were ground into the carpet, and what looked like fruit punch dripped from the couch. I turned to Ash and Jacinda. "Is it sad that this is my big first party, and all I can think about is how much cleaning will have to be done?"

Ash laughed, brushing a strand of hair away from my face. A couple in full blown make-out mode was pressed against the living room wall. When the guy came up for air, I saw the girl was Lexie, already pulling him back for more. Jacinda's eyes followed mine.

"That girl is wide open. I didn't invite her," said Jacinda. She cracked her knuckles once. "Well, you kids have fun—I gotta mingle."

Dylan returned with the drinks and whispered something in Brooklyn's ear that made her blush like the school-girl she was pretending to be. Gabriel stood in a wide stance with his arms crossed, looking more like a soldier than a teenage partier.

I nodded across the room to Curtis, who tipped his cap my way. This didn't seem to be his scene, but I was glad he was out enjoying himself. The sound of the music washed over me, and my body moved slightly to the beat. I rested against Ash, who put his arm around my waist and kissed my neck. I shut my eyes, loving the feel of his warm lips on my skin. Aside from Brooklyn and Gabriel, I didn't think I sensed any other faeries in the house. *Of course not. Any faerie with half a brain would be shut tight in their house.* Another vivid image of Corrine appeared behind my closed eyes. Corrine reached out her hand—I couldn't tell if it was in warning or greeting—and opened her mouth. A loud voice jolted me out of my daydream.

"Who cares about effin faeries anyway? Would it really be that big a loss if there weren't any?" Of course it was

Glen. Glen double-fisting beer, wearing a Nickelback T-shirt.

"I can't believe you just said that," said a girl near him. "Carrie Ann was quiet, but she was really nice. How can you justify murder?"

Glen turned my way, but then his eyes fell on Gabriel and Ash, and he turned back to the girl without saying anything to me. Thank goodness for small miracles.

"I'm just saying that I don't see what the huge deal is," Glen responded before chugging from his beer. He wiped foam from his mouth. "They're a bunch of whiners who want attention. My dad said he wouldn't be surprised if the whole serial killer deal was a hoax, so they can try and get equal rights. The thing is, they're not equal, and I know I'm not the only one that thinks it—I'm just brave enough to say it. They have *wings*, for Christ's sake."

Ash's hand curled into a fist and I pried my fingers between his until it unclenched. "Ash, don't waste your energy on this loser. Let it go."

Brooklyn, however, did not let it go. "I'm sorry, but I couldn't help overhearing you," she said, walking up to him. She stared at him with wide eyes, batting her lashes at him. "I'm surprised you don't sympathize with faeries. After all, they're a dying breed too."

Glen's eyes narrowed. "What the fuck's that mean?"

Brooklyn eyed his T-shirt. "What if it wasn't faeries being killed? What if it was people with lame-ass taste in music being oppressed, beaten, and killed? Trust me, you'd be a goner. Dumb racist."

Glen, who'd looked drunk before, now looked drunk and confused. "I'm not a racist."

"No, you're the offspring of one, but apples don't fall far, you know?" Brooklyn responded, taking a casual sip of her Diet Coke.

"Brooklyn, come here, please." I grabbed Brooklyn's arm, attempting to move her.

Ash dragged us both away, as Glen stumbled in search of a refill, muttering "crazy bitches" under his breath.

Dylan put his hand on Brooklyn's shoulder. "Look, that guy's always been a jerk. It's not worth your time." He looked at her earnestly. "I hope you don't think he represents our student body, because most of us don't think that way."

I wondered if he'd still be speaking that way if he knew what Brooklyn's shirt concealed, but then again, he seemed completely taken with her.

Brooklyn let out a deep breath. "It just makes me so mad. He's so ignorant, yet he thinks he's better than us . . . I mean . . . than faeries."

"The faerie part isn't what matters to him," said Dylan. "People like Glen compensate for their own feelings of inadequacy by acting like jerks. If it weren't faeries, it'd be another group. He only feels superior if he thinks someone else is lower than him."

Brooklyn studied Dylan. "What are you, a psychologist?"

"No, but my dad is. Apples and all, I guess." He smiled.

"He's right," said Ash. "But it's still scary that there are people like that out there. Gabe, do you . . . hey, where's Gabriel?"

I scanned the room and spotted him by the couch, his whole body tense. I caught his eye and he joined us, fury in his eyes.

"Sorry, I had to leave or I would've clocked that dickwad," Gabriel said. "Seriously, he better not come within ten feet of me."

"He could've used a clocking," said Brooklyn. She started to say something else, but then seemed to register that Dylan stood next to her.

Ash reached for my hand. "Let's go somewhere else." He leaned over and spoke quickly to Gabriel.

"Fifteen minutes," said Gabriel. "That's it, then I'm coming up there."

Ash wound his hand through mine. His expression was unreadable. We made our way through the living room and came to a staircase.

"Where are we going?" I asked, stepping over drunken bodies on the stairs.

Ash led me down the hall and stopped to check a few doors. One was unlocked, and he took me into the dark, empty bedroom. He pulled me in the room and locked the door, then pinned me to the door, twining his fingers through mine.

"Is it wrong to want a few minutes alone with my girl-friend?" asked Ash. "Especially if it's the last time we have together."

Before I could respond, his lips were on mine. I hesitated a second before giving in. I felt the intensity in his body and moved against him. I wrapped my arms around his neck, pressing myself into the heat of his skin. Ash brought his hands down to my waist, then moved them under my shirt, and worked slowly up my body. I was just getting lost in the feeling when the wind shifted.

A cold breeze from an open window in the room caressed my skin. Still kissing Ash, I opened my eyes and looked across the room out the open window. My wings buzzed beneath their bindings. I detected a faerie presence in the woods outside. Nothing was visible in the heavy darkness, but I knew someone was there. Could it be Corrine? This was what I'd been waiting for, but I had to do it alone—without endangering Ash or any of our friends. I pushed him away.

"What is it?" asked Ash. "We still have a good ten minutes before Gabriel comes banging on the door." He reached for me again, but I kept his hands at bay.

"I'm sorry. I need the bathroom. Too much Diet Coke, I guess—I'll be back in a minute. Okay?" I tried to sound as normal as possible.

"Seriously? Oh, yeah, I saw one down the hall. I'll walk you there." He reached for the doorknob.

No. He couldn't go with me. How could I get him to stay?

I pulled his arm away from the door, and gave him a seductive smile. Then I bent my head to his neck, gently nibbling it, before whispering, "I want you to save the room for us." I ran my fingers down his stomach, down over the waist of his jeans. "We can pick up where we left off."

His only response was a low moan.

I moved as quickly as I dared down the hall, then dashed down the stairs, slipped around the corner, went through the kitchen, and bolted out the back patio door.

"Hey Lila, are you even going to talk to me at all?"

Sophie sat with a group of kids on patio chairs. I skidded to a halt and surveyed the group around her.

"Come here a sec, Sophie."

Sophie flipped her hair, but got up and walked over to me. "Yes?" Her voice was like ice.

The wind picked up slightly. I had to leave. My words tumbled out in a rush. "Look, I don't have time to explain, but I have to go. You're my best friend, and you always will be—I hope you know that. But things are going on right now . . . okay, bye."

She didn't have time to respond, because I took off

through the grass toward the tree line at the edge of the backyard, leaping over several couples hooking up in the yard.

"Wait!" Sophie yelled out. "Where are you going?"

Ignoring her, I kept running. The only person near the forest edge was a guy peeing on a tree. I could just make him out in the dark, but couldn't tell who it was. I raced into the woods and stood still a minute to catch my breath. It was dark and quiet, and I tried to tune into the faerie presence I'd detected earlier.

"Lila, alone at last."

I jerked my head around. The pissing guy had been Glen, and he stood a few feet away. My body tensed. I didn't think anyone else could see me for the cover of trees. Should I step back into the light of the backyard? Would I be safer there? "What do you want, Glen?"

"Um . . ."

A slight breeze stirred, and I caught the scent of beer coming off him. "If you even think about putting so much as one finger on me again—"

He took a step closer to me. "No, I learned my lesssson." His speech was slurred. "It's juss that . . . you always acted like you were too good to even talk to me."

That's what this was all about? He thought I was stuck-up because I didn't talk enough, and he'd wanted to take me down a peg—or three? "That's why you hate me so much? Because I don't talk to you?"

Glen put his hand on a tree to steady himself. "Maybe. So how 'bout I talk to you now. And I let my hands do the talking." He took a step toward me and reached out as he stumbled.

I would have laughed at him if we weren't alone in the

woods. All I wanted was to get away from him. "Thanks, but I'm kind of with someone."

"Yeah, I don't like that guy. I'll show you what a real man is like." Glen looked around and took another step toward me. "What are you doing in the woods by yourself anyway? Are you alone?"

Panic rose in my chest. "I, uh, just needed some time to myself. Oh, some girl was just asking about you in the party . . . blond hair, she said you were cute. She was looking for you."

He stood there a minute, as though unsure of himself, then veered back toward Jacinda's backyard. "Okay, I better find out who it is."

I nodded, turned back toward the trees, and took off farther into the forest. Stars twinkled above. The bright orb of the moon lit up the forest floor where it broke through the trees. I took a breath and closed my eyes, trying to pinpoint the other faerie. He or she was close. *Please let it be Corrine.* As I opened my eyes, the shadow of a large, black cloud crept across the sky, masking the glow of the moon. Everything was immersed in darkness. It looked exactly like the woods from my recurring dream.

My senses drew me deeper into the woods. My brain screamed at me to stop—hadn't I learned anything from the few horror movies I'd allowed Sophie to drag me to see? *Scary Movie Rule #1: Don't wander alone in dark, scary woods.* No matter what happened, at least Ash and the others would be safe. Hopefully, it would end with me, and no one else would die. I gazed behind me but could no longer see the bright lights of the house. *Good-bye, Ash Cooper.* I turned to face my fate.

HAPPILY EVER AFTER

I am almost giddy with excitement. *The One is coming to me. Finally, I will kill Lila Kincade, and it will be the beginning of the end. My heroic legacy will be sealed: tonight marks the night I save mankind. It's true what they say, you know—hard work does pay off.*

WAKING DREAMS

With the moon shrouded behind the cloud's veil, I had only the strange sensations in my gut and wings to guide me. I shivered in the cold, damp air, wishing I'd brought a coat as I navigated deeper into the woods. Ash had to have noticed I was gone by now. I quickened my pace, wanting to put as much distance as possible between us.

Twigs and leaves crunched under my feet, and I cringed at the sound. If only I could fly, but I didn't have time to unbind myself—and I didn't particularly want to be topless when I faced my killer. Following the sense of the other faerie in the woods, I felt drawn as if to a homing device, more strongly as I ventured farther into the forest.

I stopped to listen. *What was that?* A twig snapped nearby. Frozen in place, I tried to quiet my breathing, which was coming in ragged gasps. *Snap.* There it was again, closer. My fingers tightened around the pepper spray in my pocket. Why hadn't I brought the knife with me? Ash had the gun *and* the knife with him. *Brilliant.* Not that I could have asked him for the knife without arousing suspicion, but still.

Squinting in the blackness, I saw the outline of a small building in front of me. Taking a few hesitant steps closer, I caught my breath. I knew without a doubt that if the moon lit up the area, the shack would look identical to one in my dream. The nightmare that always ended with me about to die. I pushed through the last few trees surrounding the shack. The sense of the other faerie overwhelmed me—or was it more than one? With a deep breath, I took a step out into the clearing.

A hand gripped my shoulder from behind, while another clamped over my mouth, stifling my scream.

"Lila, sshhh, it's me," Ash whispered frantically. "Don't scream."

I tried to contain my terror in a whisper. "What are you doing here?"

Ash didn't let go of my arm. "I was looking out the window while I waited for you, and I saw you run into the woods. Why would you come out here by yourself?"

"I wanted to save you." I put a finger to my lips, gesturing toward the cabin ahead of them. Every hair on the back of my neck tingled, and my wings strained against their bindings. My fight-or-flight response had kicked into high gear, and my body was clearly picking the flight option.

I stared at the dilapidated structure in front of us. *Scary Movie Rule #2: Don't investigate creepy shacks.*

Ash gulped. "You want to go in there?"

"No, but we have to. This is the place I've been dreaming about."

"The nightmares you told me about? Great. Guess we're prepared, at least." Ash reached for his gun.

I squeezed his hand, then let go. Ash held the gun with one hand, and twisted the door handle with the other. It wasn't locked.

The door creaked open and I stiffened. "Ready?" I whispered.

Ash nodded and flung the door open. The shrieking hinges sounded like a dying cat. *We are so not making a quiet entrance.* We waited a moment, but I heard nothing aside from our own frantic breathing.

I reached inside, fumbling for the light switch. There was none. As my eyes adjusted to the blackness of the cabin, I spotted a bare bulb hanging from the ceiling in the middle of the room. I tapped Ash on the shoulder and pointed at it.

Keeping the gun raised in front of him, Ash stepped through the doorway and moved to the center of the room. He pulled the cord and dim wattage from the bulb cast flickering shadows over the walls. The shack appeared abandoned, save for a small table and an old weathered couch on the far wall. But the high-alert status reverberating through my body said otherwise. That looks were deceiving.

"It's still creepy with the light on," Ash whispered.

About to follow Ash into the shack, I stumbled, overcome with dizziness and nausea. I pivoted and vomited onto the ground by the door. I wiped my mouth on my sleeve, then ran into the room and gripped Ash's arm.

"That's not a good sign, is it?" Ash asked.

I shook my head and pointed at a single door on the right side of the room.

"Must be the bedroom," said Ash. He looked at me. "Let me guess. We need to go in there too."

"Yes." I groaned. *Scary Movie Rule #3: Psychos love to hide in dark places.*

Ash tried the door. It was locked from the inside. He pushed harder. It didn't budge.

Ash took a step back, then charged, throwing his shoulder into the door, which made a cracking sound.

Another hard strike and the door gave way. I flinched, one hand on the pepper spray. My head buzzed with searing, sharp pain and renewed sickness swept through my stomach. I grasped Ash's arm.

Ash reached toward the light cord and a pale glow filled the small room. Closed black curtains hung from the lone window. Ash staggered backward, the gun shaking along with his hand. I stared in horror.

Faerie wings were pinned to the walls, most of them covered in blood. It looked like an insane giant's version of a butterfly collection. A bloody bed sat in the dead center of the room.

"Lila."

I turned to the left side of the room. It was Mr. Finch, hunched over, vomiting onto the floor. He was alive and he was unbound, his wings beating behind him. I headed toward him, checking to make sure no one else was in the room.

"Mr. Finch! Are you okay? We have to get out of here . . ." My voice trailed off as I took another step, and he stood up. I looked down at his hands.

"Do you like my work, Lila?" Mr. Finch asked. He held a knife and a pair of lavender wings that dripped fresh blood. I was close enough now that I saw a lifeless male faerie on the floor. He placed the wings and knife carefully on the bed. "I get sick too, just like you, but it's worth it."

I gaped at Mr. Finch. His wings were a darkish gray. I'd never seen gray wings before, but they didn't look like a solid gray. It was as if they had dulled over time, like they had once been . . .

"Yes, I'm just as special as you are, so you can stop staring now," Mr. Finch said.

Ash raised the gun and aimed for the center of Mr.

Finch's head. Mr. Finch flew up and behind Ash in a blur. Before Ash could fire, Mr. Finch picked him up by the shirt and threw him against the wall.

"No!" I cried. Ash moaned and slumped to the ground. Chuckling, Mr. Finch retrieved the gun from Ash's limp hand and emptied the bullets onto the floor before tossing it across the room. He was too fast. Also too strong. He had figured out his own magic long before I had. Some kind of super-strength, super-speed thing. I remembered the dreams where something had torn the wings off the faeries with blinding speed. The wings I'd heard beating in the last dream hadn't been of a faerie coming to help me . . . they'd been his.

He reached me in an instant with the knife and cut my shirt and bindings up the back in one swift motion. My wings spread out around me, my shirt barely hanging on in front. I backed away from him, but he laughed and landed right in front of me. He leaned in close, studying my wings.

"But, Mr. Finch, you're a faerie too. Why?" I asked, before a darker question floated in my mind. "Oh God, are you my . . . my . . . ?"

"No, you stupid creature, I'm not your father. Your father was weak. He loved Stella. He was oh-so-excited about your imminent birth." Mr. Finch clasped his hands in mock glee, gesturing at the wall. "His wings are those pretty clear ones on the left."

I squeezed my eyes shut to stop the tears. So the dream about my dead father had been real. The room was spinning. "And my mother?" I asked, wishing this were still only a nightmare.

Mr. Finch grimaced. "Stella wasn't dumb, I'll give her that. That whole trick of leaving you with a human to raise you. I followed her for a while but soon realized there was no child with her. Then I had a dream." He studied my face. "Did you know Pure Ones often have psychic dreams?"

Though I'd been figuring that out, I shook my head no.

Finch continued. "I dreamed of a school in Chapel Hill. When I saw Northeast, I felt a pull to be there. So I became a teacher. I had to wait sixteen years, but as you can see, I've kept myself occupied." He nodded toward his grotesque wall art.

Ash still lay sprawled by the wall. My heart hammered in my chest as I considered taking the mace from my pocket. With Mr. Finch's agility and strength, he'd likely take it from me before I had the chance to use it. I needed more time. I needed Ash to wake up.

I gulped. "How long have you known it was me?"

He paused. "A little over a week ago, I sensed a surge of faerie magic in the school, which could mean only one thing: the Pure One was falling in love, and their power was being awakened." He yawned elaborately. "So I killed as many faeries as I could in the surrounding area to decrease the Pure One's power while I figured out who it was."

Ash remained motionless. *Wake up*, I screamed in my head. But of course, he didn't. I couldn't command people the way I could bells.

Finch continued, "I had to be sure, you understand. If I killed a Pure One, I'd kill myself as well."

He watched me, taking one step closer. "By the lack of surprise on your face, I'm guessing you already knew that. Interesting." Evil saturated his voice, and I shivered. "I knew you'd be drawn to other faeries, especially one you had an emotional attachment with. So I got one of those, hoping she'd draw you to come to play with me."

"Corrine," I said. No wonder Corrine had been prominent in my mind the past few days.

Finch came even closer, turning his face to the light. An angry, red gash was visible down his cheek. "She's a fighter. She is by far the most . . . troublesome . . . I've encountered."

Is. He said she *is* a fighter, not *was.* She was alive. Corrine must've loved digging her hot pink nails into his face.

Finch ran his middle finger down the cut. "Trust me, I told her that once I drew you here, I would kill her very slowly."

Thoughts flew through my head in a rush, but were jumbled by fear. *Come on, math brain, kick in and solve this.*

Finch pulled out a long knife from his jacket and flipped it back and forth in his hand, the blade glinting in the low light.

"You never answered the why part," I said.

He looked up from the knife in surprise. "Why? That's easy. Half-faeries are nothing—no better than humans. Their inter-mating has spoiled what it means to be a true faerie." He spat at the ground. "It's my job to clean up the mess left behind. We should rule over humans, not fraternize with them."

What? "Why didn't you just go back to the realm yourself all those years ago?"

Finch's eyes gleamed like cold glass. Hatred burned in them. "Once upon a time, my magic awoke, the same way as yours did. That's right—I was in love once, with a human. Then she found out I was a faerie, and it was like I had leprosy instead of wings. She didn't care a whit about the difference between Pure and half-faerie—she was repulsed by me." He slammed his fist into the wall. "She was wrong. Pure ones are superior beings to all. Those diluted half-wits have no real power other than flitting around with their garish colored wings. The magnificence of our heritage cannot shine as long as they are around. We can be what we once were."

Winged murderers who wanted to conquer the planet?

He eyed me. "But I knew there was only one on Earth who could stop me . . . one as powerful as I am. The offspring of Stella Ambrose."

I was running out of time, and Ash still wasn't moving. I tried to stall. "What about the wings on eBay?"

Finch grimaced. "It's hard to wipe out an entire species on a teacher's salary."

I couldn't believe his betrayal to his own kind . . . my kind. Or his narcissism. My wings surged with energy and, despite the circumstances, felt strong and free.

Mr. Finch took another step toward me. A trickle of blood ran down the knife. "Look at the bright side, Lila." His face was now inches from mine. "At least you don't have to worry about doing that next essay."

I tried to step back. "But, you can't kill me or you'll die too. You said so yourself."

His wings beat behind him a moment, and he hovered in front of me before grabbing my arm and lifting me in the air as if I were a feather. He was unbelievably strong. He laughed as he flew us outside and around the back of the shack. "Don't worry. I'm not going to kill you myself. Someone is going to do it for me."

43

MAGIC

Finch landed, his arm still gripping me, and used his foot to sweep leaves away from the ground, uncovering a small door. I struggled against him, trying to break free, but his fingers dug into the flesh of my arm. He pulled the rusty door open with his other hand, revealing a vast blackness beyond it. Finch jerked my wrist, pulling me behind him as we flew down into the space. My wings flapped in a desperate, futile attempt to fly away from his iron grip. When we reached the floor, about nine feet down, Finch roughly tied my hands behind my back and shoved me backward, into the shadowy depths of the tomb-like room. The scent of damp earth invaded my nostrils.

The door slammed shut above me and silence enveloped the room. Was he gone? A small click preceded a beam from a flashlight, flooding the small space. So much for hoping he'd left. The light revealed two faeries huddled together, against the far wall. It took a moment for me to realize that one of them was Corrine, her blond hair more streaked with mud than pink, her face covered in scratches and bruises. However, as soon as our eyes locked, I saw the same familiar spark in them.

Next to Corrine was a faerie who looked a few years younger than me. She was as grubby as Corrine, but her eyes were vacant. Their wings were bound, their hands apparently tied behind them.

"Kellie Jo, this is what you've been waiting for," said Finch. He cut the ties off the faerie's hands and unbound her wings. "Do this one thing for me, and you will be free."

The faerie stared ahead, blankly. Her face was familiar, but I couldn't place it. Finch had to snap his fingers near her face to bring her back to the moment.

"Come here, Kellie Jo. Remember this?" he asked, as he held the knife in front of her.

"Don't do it, honey. He's never going to let you go no matter what he says," said Corrine.

Finch shook with anger. "I would kill you now, except that I want you to watch Lila die first."

Kellie Jo took a hesitant step toward Finch. "I'll really get to go home to my sister?"

Finch smiled. "I promise you will be with your sister very soon."

That's when it struck me. Mr. Finch liked insurance policies. I bet this was Carrie Ann's little sister—I'd seen her several times with her mother in the school parking lot. And Kellie Jo had no idea that her sister was already dead.

In a quiet but sure voice, I said, "He already killed your sister, Kellie Jo. He did it during school today."

Kellie Jo sobbed, staring at Finch in horror. "You murdered my sister?"

Finch flew at me lightning fast and backhanded me across the face. I stumbled and fell over sideways, almost landing on Corrine. As I struggled to stand, Corrine whispered, "Remember who you are."

Finch grabbed Kellie Jo, shoving the handle of the knife in her hand. "Here's the deal, Tinker Bell," he said. "If you want to go home to Mommy, you must kill Lila." He squeezed her hand, forcing her fingers to bend around the knife. "If you don't, I'll kill you instead." Finch shone the flashlight in my face.

Kellie Jo held the knife, her hand trembling. She looked at me and gasped, staring at my wings. "They're so beautiful," she whispered.

"Now, Kellie Jo," Finch ordered calmly.

Kellie Jo paused for a second, then raised the knife and ran toward me.

I closed my eyes. *Holy hell, this is it.*

They say when a person dies, their life flashes before their eyes. What flashed before mine were dreams—all the ones I'd had since this started. Dreams of dark woods, the ocean, storms, and faeries. Hundreds of faeries. Looking to me to help them. "Use your magic," one whispered, before fading away. *Yeah, I'd love to, but there are no bells here.*

I opened my eyes as Kellie Jo jabbed the knife at me. I rose off the ground and flew unsteadily to the left, my balance off as my hands were tied.

"No, Kellie Jo!" Corrine screamed, attempting to stand.

Finch flew to Corrine, pushing her hard back down to the ground. Kellie Jo flew at me again, tears streaming down her face. I darted to the side, but I couldn't move away from the knife in time. It sliced my right shoulder, and blood oozed down my back.

Finch groaned. He might be strong, but he couldn't stop himself from being impacted if another faerie was hurt. And maybe it was worse that I was a Pure One like him. *If only he were a telephone—or a remote control.*

And then it clicked. I couldn't control people, but I could make the phone ring and the television louder because they weren't living things. They were just things. I might not have power over the deranged man in front of me, but maybe I could control any inanimate object. Acknowledging this possibility, my wings responded by blazing brighter than ever before.

Kellie Jo, who had been flying toward me in the small space, stopped midair, shielding her eyes from the blinding glare. I willed my bindings to untie from my hands and felt them loosen and fall away. Elation coursed through me—I'd been right about the nature of my gift. I focused on the glint of the knife and willed it out of Kellie Jo's hand. Kellie Jo screeched in surprise as the knife floated out of her grasp.

I might not be able to kill Finch myself, but I sure wanted to cause some serious harm. I forced the knife to change direction, and it veered in the air toward Finch. The knife sailed through the air and caught him in the left wing, pinning him back into the dirt wall behind him. A searing pain tore through my own left wing the moment the knife hit him. He struggled, but the knife had gone in deep, and I could tell he didn't want to tear through his wing.

Ignoring my own pain, I willed the flashlight to connect with Finch's face, its beam illuminating the blood that trickled from his nose where it hit. I almost enjoyed the throbbing in my own nose. Kelli Jo had landed in the far corner of the room. She was curled up on the floor in a fetal position, bawling.

I willed Corrine's bindings to come undone just as Ash dropped down from the opening above. The entire area glowed in the light of my wings, and his eyes lit up when he saw Corrine alive on the floor. Unfortunately, he landed right where Finch was pinned to the wall. Finch's hand shot out and closed around Ash's throat. Ash quickly tossed something across the small space to me. It was my kitchen knife.

Finch laughed and turned to me, his hand still on Ash's throat. "It's not like you can kill me, Lila."

I looked at Corrine, and she nodded slightly. Confusion crossed Finch's face as I tossed the knife to her. She flew up to catch the knife, her wrist bindings falling to the ground, then soared straight at Finch. "She can't kill you," Corrine confirmed, driving the knife straight into his heart, "but I can."

I screamed in pain as Finch's heart was pierced, and Finch released his hold on Ash, who stumbled but quickly regained his footing. He helped Corrine push Finch around to face the wall, his pinned wing twisted behind him. Corrine sliced through the seracord, separating his wings from his body in one quick stroke. As blood gushed out onto the dirt, Ash shoved him back against the wall.

"Collect this, psycho," Ash said, throwing Finch's own wing at him.

44

AFTERMATH

I fell to my knees, gagging and puking at the same time. Unbelievable that Finch's death made me physically ill. He didn't deserve my sickness. My wings dimmed for a few seconds, then regained their high wattage gleam.

Corrine stood, dropping the knife like it was diseased and wiping her bloody hands on the dirt wall. "I never want to have to do that ever again." She turned to Ash with tired eyes. "It sure is good to see you, little bro."

Ash embraced his sister in a tight hug. "I thought you were dead."

"I'm alive and kickin', thanks to your girlfriend here," said Corrine, looking over at me. "You did a great job . . . I knew you'd figure the magic part out." Her eyes dropped to where blood still dripped from my shoulder. She flew to me. "Oh honey, are you okay?"

"I think so," I said, though I was still unsteady on my feet. "I'm just glad you're alive. I kept seeing flashes of you in my mind, but I wasn't sure why."

Ash reached my side, and I grabbed him. "You, too—I was going crazy when Finch threw you up there."

Ash's arms encircled my waist, though he was careful not to touch my shoulder. "Thanks, but it's because of you, my sister didn't die. Because of you, it's over."

"Well, because of you, we had an extra knife," I said. "You have amazing timing, by the way."

"I helped, but you saved us all. Without you, nothing would have stopped him." Ash kissed me tenderly. "I think I'm a little in love with you, Lila Kincade."

I smiled. "I think I'm okay with that."

"Aw, that makes a girl's heart melt," Corrine said. "But let's get out of this hole in the ground."

Soft sobs caught my attention. Kellie Jo was still curled up in a ball in the corner. We cautiously approached her, and I touched her arm. "Kellie Jo?"

Kellie Jo wailed louder. "I'm so, so, so sorry. I was afraid —I didn't want to die. But now I wish I was dead. I want to be with my sister."

I knelt down beside her. "I know you only did it because you felt you had no choice. I'm so sorry about Carrie Ann." At some point, I'd tell her about how I was with Carrie Ann when she died, but now wasn't the right time.

Kellie Jo cried even harder. I let her cry for a few minutes, with my arm around her. Her tears soaked my shirt, which hung in tatters around me. "Are you ready to get out of here?" I asked.

She sniffled and nodded. My wings dimmed to a steady glow. Kellie Jo flew in front of us, and Corrine and I flew Ash up and out of the opening. I avoided looking at my dead teacher, but I knew the image of that bloodstained winged wall in the cabin would stay with me forever.

We landed near the shack to regroup, while Kellie Jo tried to compose herself. At least her parents would have some comfort in the fact that one of their children was alive.

I hadn't even heard she'd been missing, but maybe that was on purpose. Ash let Kellie Jo use his cell phone to call her parents before he called his mom, and despite being a foot from the phone, I heard his mom burst into tears as soon as Ash put Corrine on the phone.

Leaving the forest would be tricky, given that three of us had wings and mine glowed in a steady way that I figured was their new normal state. While we weighed out our options, the forest came alive behind us. Gabriel burst into the clearing with his gun drawn, Brooklyn at his side. They were followed by Ms. Gable, and my next-door neighbor, Mrs. Nesbaum. I was floored to see they both had wings. Another man with them also had a gun pointed in front of him.

"What the—?" exclaimed Gabriel, staring at Corrine. "No flippin' way." He picked up Corrine with one arm, his gun in the other hand, and kissed her quickly on the mouth. Corrine looked shocked but not unhappy as he put her down. Gabriel turned toward us and simply asked, "What the hell?"

"Sorry, big guy," said Ash. "I saw Lila going into the woods and ran to find her. You were too far away. You wouldn't have heard me yell over the music."

Brooklyn looked at her friends and then at the cabin. "Oh, thank God. You guys okay?" she asked, hugging me.

"I think so," I said. We gave everyone a brief description of what had happened, including the recent murder of the faerie in the cabin bedroom. The man with the gun nodded and headed inside. The dark cloud had drifted away, and the bright aura from the stars and moon lit up the night around them. We huddled in a tight circle by the shack, though I refused to look in the direction of all those wings.

"So it *was* Finch," said Ms. Gable.

"You knew?" I asked. "Did you know about me, too?"

Ms. Gable shook her head. "No, I don't have the sensing ability of Pure Ones—I just had a hunch. Ella here confirmed it." Ms. Gable gestured toward Mrs. Nesbaum—whose name was Nellie, not Ella, but Ms. Gable was close. "Also, I noticed Mr. Finch watching you at your locker. Something seemed wrong with it."

I gazed at Mrs. Nesbaum in astonishment. My nosy next-door neighbor was a faerie? "You knew about me all along?" I asked her.

Mrs. Nesbaum smiled. "You probably don't remember this, Lila, but one day when you were five years old, you decided to have a little excursion around your backyard."

I was shocked. "You saw that? So you also saw my clear wings. But Mrs. Nesbaum, why didn't you tell my mother? I mean—you're a faerie too."

"Guilty as charged, dear. And now that you know, you may call me Ella."

"Ella? Wait, not . . . Ella Tatiana, author of *Confessions of a Real-Life Faerie*?" She nodded. "But . . . you were supposed to be in exile."

Mrs. Nesbaum laughed. "Well, some would say this town *is* exile compared to New York City."

I eyed her. "So the whole practically-deaf-and-blind thing was an act?"

Mrs. Nesbaum grinned. "It was preferable to have others think I was incapacitated. It helped me look after you better."

"Unbelievable." I shook my head.

"I knew your mother treasured her privacy, as I did mine. That doesn't mean I didn't keep a careful eye on you, especially recently. I'm head of the local advocacy group for faeries here." Mrs. Nesbaum—Ella—patted my hand. "You were getting to the age when I was about to ask you to join our group anyway."

I smiled at her. "Were these advocacy meetings run at your house?"

"Yes. Ann . . . Ms. Gable and I had been meeting in secret every month, but we met more often when the murders started," said Mrs. Nesbaum.

"That was your car in front of her house, then?" I asked, looking at my math teacher.

Ms. Gable nodded. "My job in the group has always been to protect faeries, but once we suspected you were in trouble, we monitored your every move."

"I felt like I was being watched," I said, "but usually not in a good way."

"He was watching you too," said Ms. Gable.

The man with the gun came out of the cabin then, giving rapid orders into his phone. He came over to us and offered me his hand. "Ms. Kincade, Agent Heinrichsen. I've been following this case for some time. We've been working with Mrs. Nesbaum here for the last two weeks." He paused and looked at Ash. "Mr. Cooper, I'm the one who's been in contact with your mother about this young lady here." He put his hand out to Corrine. "I can't tell you how happy I am to see you're okay."

Corrine hesitated a second but then shook his hand. "Thanks."

He laughed. "I understand your distrust of the government, but some of us have actually been working around the clock to find this guy. I thought about some guy targeting my daughter. I haven't slept in a week."

"Is my mom okay?" I asked.

Heinrichsen nodded. "Yes, we've had a team staked out at the house all day."

"It's true," said Mrs. Nesbaum. "Apparently our organization isn't quite as secret as I'd hoped, but Agent Heinrichsen has been nothing but helpful. When I saw you leave your house tonight, we followed you here, and he met up with us on the way. Unfortunately, we lost track of you for a bit at the party."

I blushed, remembering the bedroom and my disappearing act.

Corrine reached up, touching the dirt caked in her hair. "Can we get out of this godforsaken place now? I'm dying to take a shower."

Heinrichsen chuckled. "Young lady, you're exactly how you appeared on television. You certainly won't be forgotten by several members of the Philadelphia police force."

"Good," said Corrine, beaming.

"Let's go," said Heinrichsen. "We'll get you back to your car. Don't worry about being seen; we cleared everyone out of there. I'll follow you home, and we'll get some quick statements. My guys are en route now to set up a perimeter and do their thing here."

We set out back the way we'd come through the trees. I held tight to Ash's hand, my wings waving gently in the night air. The clouds had dissipated, leaving the moon unscathed in their wake. Moonlight washed the woods, and the forest took on a subtle glow. My wings added their own luminosity to guide us to the edge of the trees.

A low whistle escaped from Mrs. Nesbaum. "Those are some gorgeous wings, dearie. I've never seen the likes of 'em before."

Heinrichsen cleared his throat. "They're spectacular."

"Thanks," I said. I hesitated at the tree line with the others. If the party was still going, I'd be seen for what I was.

The lights from an army of police cars permeated the

backyard. No worries that anyone was still hanging around. Police streamed through the area with flashlights and headed toward the shack.

Ash squeezed my hand. "I'll cover you with my coat. We'll try to get you to the car without anyone seeing you."

I took a deep breath. "Nope. I'm not hiding my wings anymore."

"Good for you, honey. I'm with you," said Corrine, taking my other hand.

"We're with you too, dear," said Ms. Gable, who winked at Mrs. Nesbaum.

"Are you sure?" asked Heinrichsen. "If you all do this, you can't go back. Everyone will know what you are."

I'd never been so sure. "Good, let them know."

I raised my head, and my wings fluttered behind me, their glow creating a strobe-light effect in the darkness. With Ash and Corrine on either side, I stepped out of the woods and into the light.

EPILOGUE

"Stop fidgeting, I'm trying to finish your hair," Brooklyn said. She sprayed another lock into submission. "There. Okay, you can look now."

I faced the full-length mirror and stared in shock at the reflection staring back. Brooklyn had managed to tame my defiant locks into smooth, dark waves that fell over my shoulders. The silver dress skimmed my body, perfectly accented by my shimmering wings.

"That dress was made for your wings—or vice versa," said Brooklyn.

"Thanks. You look amazing too," I said. "Dylan's gonna love that dress."

Brooklyn admired her own much shorter dress. Her ice-blue wings contrasted the dark violet of the dress. "I think he's gonna love my legs."

There was a tap on the door, and Sophie, looking radiant in a pale blue strapless dress, stepped in. "This is going to be the best night ever."

"Sophie! You look amazing! Thank you so much for coming over." I gave her a hug and looked her in the eye. "I know I said it before, but I'm so sorry I didn't tell you . . . about me."

Brooklyn looked skeptical. "Did you really not know?"

"Oh, I knew. We've best friends forever, and we've played together since we were little kids. I saw the bandages on her back a few times when we were young. I didn't know what they were, so I asked my mom."

My eyes went wide. "Wait, what? Your mom knew too? You didn't tell me that."

Sophie nodded. "She asked me to describe the bandages, and I said that you always wore them. I'm not gonna lie, she freaked at first. But she really likes you, and told me not to make it a big deal. So I didn't."

"I still don't get why didn't you say something," I said.

Sophie shrugged. "I figured you'd tell me when you were ready. It didn't change anything for me. But you totally owe me a movie . . . and you might have to bring a blanket or something, so your wings don't light up the theater."

I laughed. "Deal. Can you believe we're going to a formal? A week ago, I didn't think I'd even be alive."

"I know," said Brooklyn. "Life is one wild ride, and I'm glad we get to stay on it a little longer."

The doorbell rang, and the three of us took one last look in the mirror and headed for the stairs.

Ash gaped up at me. "Wow," was all he managed.

Dylan stared at Brooklyn. "What he said."

Curtis swooped into a low bow. "Breathtaking, miladies." Sophie and I looked at each other and giggled.

After Mom gushed over all of us and took a bazillion pictures, she stared at my wings with tears in her eyes. "You look beautiful. I'm so happy you can be yourself." She snif-fled. "I can't believe my little girl has grown up so fast."

"Oh, Mom," I said, giving her a quick hug. "I love you. I'll be home by . . . oh yeah, when is my curfew?" I had never needed one before.

I WALKED into the gym with my wings on full display and Ash at my side. I'd spent my entire life avoiding the spotlight and was now smack in the center of it. A camera crew hovered around and filmed me walking into school like it was national news—which it was. The turmoil was compounded when Ms. Gable appeared, also without her bindings. We left the protesters in the parking lot behind us, where Glen led chants of "Faerie freaks go home!"

The gym was surreal. It had been transformed by gold and navy balloons. Ms. Gable gave us a thumbs-up as she walked off to join Mr. Turner.

One boy by the door stared openly at my wings. "Dude —you're glowing."

I stood a little taller and lifted my chin. "Yeah, I guess I am."

"Cool," said the boy.

A jumble of classmates danced in the center of the room. Sure, they'd gawked at me for a second, but then went right back to enjoying the music. I hoped that the rest of the world would follow suit. The band started playing a slow song.

Ash held out his hand. "Dance with me?"

"I thought you'd never ask," I teased.

Under the bluish haze of the gym lights, I danced with Ash in contented silence until the song's end. I leaned back and arched my eyebrow at Ash. "There is one thing that would make me even happier—if you're up for it."

A devilish grin appeared on his face.

I rolled my eyes. "Not that . . . not yet." I tugged him by the arm out the back door of the gym. The night was quiet and still.

"What are we doing out here?" asked Ash. He tried to pull me toward him, but I danced out of his reach.

"I want you to watch me." I said. "I've wanted to do this for so long now."

With only Ash and the stars as witnesses, I did what I hadn't done for fun since I was five years old.

I flew.

ACKNOWLEDGMENTS

This book is close to my heart for several reasons. After my sci-fi books were published by Egmont USA, my extremely supportive husband congratulated me and celebrated with me, but then confessed that his favorite book of mine was still "the one about the serial killer and faeries." It had been the first book I'd written and had been relegated to a long forgotten file on my laptop. I rediscovered my love for Lila's story and began the process of re-writing it. So a huge thank you to my husband for believing that Lila's story needed to be told. Also, thanks to Becca, Mike, and Tracy for being willing to read anything at the drop of a hat, and to Dad, for always asking for the next book.

I have to thank the earliest readers of The Wing Collector by my first critique partners: Jeanne Ryan, Niki Schoenfeldt, Kelly Dyksterhouse, Joanne Zakula, Mary Louise Sanchez, Lacey Boldyrev and Valerie Kemp who gave me the determination to keep going in this crazy business. Thank you to the Linger Ladies: Aimee Henley, Rebecca Taylor, and Shawn McGuire for their endless supply of support, knowledge and laughter, and who have inspired me to write more short stories, like Wingless, the prequel to this novel.

A huge thanks to my amazing editor, Maya Myers, who helped make this book what I hoped it could be. I feel so thankful to have her incredible talent in my corner. Also, thank you to cover designer extraordinaire, Steven Novak, for the haunting cover image that captured the North Carolina woods perfectly. It's probably the writer in me, but every time I'm back in North Carolina driving on those twisty, wooded roads, I think it's beautiful—and also the perfect place for a serial killer to hide out.

Finally, thank you to all the awesome readers who found this book and allowed me to take you on Lila's journey. Please sign up for my **author newsletter** for new release updates and giveaways **here,** or on my website at kristihelvig.com, and you will get Wingless as a gift. I hope you enjoyed the ride and if so, please consider leaving a review which is a great way to help authors! Until next time.

Peace and love,
Kristi

EXCEPT FROM KILLER POINTE

Ballerina by day. Assassin by night.

Read an excerpt from the new urban fantasy novel, Killer Pointe, from Dark Edge Publishing. An aspiring professional dancer plans to fund her dreams of attending Juilliard School in this world by serving as a killer-for-hire in a parallel fairy tale world.

She was prettier than me. They all were. She laid very still, her long golden hair fanned out over the satin pillowcase. I crept closer. Her skin shone like flawless ivory; her lips pink as roses. I hoped I wasn't too late. No, there it was, the slight rise and fall of her chest. She was alive.

A slight breeze stirred the clouds and a sliver of moonlight escaped, lighting up part of the tower room through the window. I glanced outside. The tiny opening led to such an expansive, yet unreachable view. How sad.

I headed back down one flight of stairs. The scent of rain clung to the air and dampness permeated the stones in the wall. A lantern would give me away, so I used my hands for guidance.

My feet were nimble, and I grazed one of the slick stones with my shoulder. It couldn't be much farther.

I reached the landing and hesitated. My heart raced like it always did when I got to this part. I moved down the hallway and guessed this particular door would be locked. It was.

I reached in my pocket and pulled out my trusty lock-picker. A nice perk of the shifting was that I always landed here with my work gear, aka, a sword and small pick attached to my traditional tunic and leggings. After fiddling with the lock a minute, I was rewarded with a click. I put my ear to the door and turned the knob. It opened with a slight creak and I froze but relaxed at the sound of heavy snoring. This one didn't feel the need for guards like some of the others. I leapt to her bedside and in one smooth movement, unsheathed my jeweled sword.

Her white hair stuck out in curls around her head and wrinkles sunk deep into her face. A smile played at her lips, as though she dreamed of sweets and puppies. She almost looked like someone's kind, if somewhat eccentric, grandmother. Almost.

I plunged the sword deep into the woman's chest. Her eyes flew open and she gasped once, her gnarled hands clawing at the weapon. I pushed the sword in deeper and her hands fell to her sides, her eyes still open but no longer seeing.

After placing coins on her eyelids, I wiped my sword clean and raced down the remaining stairs, out into the night. The cloud cover had dissipated, and stars twinkled in the brisk air. I ran back toward the forest where the Queen's horse waited for me but glanced back at the tower room.

"Don't worry, princess," I whispered. "Your prince will come."

Read KILLER POINTE now.

ABOUT THE AUTHOR

Kristi Helvig is a Ph.D. clinical psychologist turned sci-fi/fantasy author. Her debut sci-fi novel, BURN OUT (Egmont USA/Lerner Publishing), was called "a scorching series opener not to be missed." Her latest book, *KILLER POINTE* (Dark Edge Publishing) is an urban fantasy involving a teen who plans to fund her dream of attending Juilliard School for dance in this world by serving as a paid assassin in a parallel fairy tale world. Kristi muses about Star Trek, space monkeys, and other assorted topics at www.kristihelvig.com and on Twitter (@KristiHelvig). Kristi resides in sunny Colorado with her hubby, two kiddos, and behaviorally-challenged dogs.

ALSO BY KRISTI HELVIG

Killer Pointe

The Missing

The Boy Who Wasn't There

Countdown Cafe

Burn Out (re-releasing Summer 2020)

Strange Skies (re-releasing Summer 2020)

The House on 6th Street (coming Fall 2020)

www.ingramcontent.com/pod-product-compliance
Lightning Source LLC
Chambersburg PA
CBHW021233250626
47155CB00008B/2994